THE
LONGEST
Pleasure

THE
LONGEST
Pleasure

DOUGLAS CLARK

PERENNIAL LIBRARY
Harper & Row, Publishers
New York, Cambridge, Philadelphia, San Francisco
London, Mexico City, São Paulo, Sydney

A hardcover edition of this book was published in 1981 by Victor Gollancz Ltd., London, England. It is here reprinted by arrangement with John Farquharson, Ltd.

First PERENNIAL LIBRARY edition published 1984.

Library of Congress Cataloging in Publication Data

Clark, Douglas.
  The longest pleasure.

  Reprint. Originally published: New York : Morrow, 1981.
  "Perennial library."
  I. Title.
[PR6053.L294L6 1984]   823'.914   83-48335
ISBN 0-06-080689-3 (pbk.)

84 85 86 87 88 10 9 8 7 6 5 4 3 2 1

Now hatred is by far the longest pleasure;
Men love in haste, but they detest at leisure.
                              Byron: *Don Juan*

Chapter 1

DETECTIVE CHIEF SUPERINTENDENT George Masters dropped
the two or three feet from the promenade edge on to the sand and
turned to help his wife down. Wanda was, by now, heavily preg-
nant, and Masters was taking even greater care of her than usual.
He put up his long arms and lifted her down bodily. As he did so,
he heard the shout.

"Hoy! Hoy!"

As Wanda made sure her voluminous coat was properly settled
after her somewhat unceremonious descent, Masters turned in the
direction from which the shout had come. Shambling at a half-run
towards them was a policeman, hampered in his progress by the
softness of the sand and the rubber boots he was wearing.

Masters had taken a few days of the leave owing to him to bring
Wanda away for a last break before she had her child. It was early
spring. The Isle of Wight was practically deserted. They had been
able to enjoy the solitude and the strolls along the water's edge in
the bright, breezy weather. Wrapped up warmly, Wanda had
enjoyed the wind playing through her hair and the sense of freedom the solitude had given her. Each day they had taken this same
walk and Masters had been highly pleased at his wife's enjoyment
and her obvious good health and well-being. But today—their last
full day—it seemed they were not to be left entirely alone to enjoy
their slow saunter.

"Hoy!" The policeman was waving his arms as if to shoo them
off the beach and up again on to the promenade.

"You can't come along here, sir," puffed the constable as he
came up. "You'll have to get off the front altogether."

"May I ask why, Constable?"

"No, you may not, sir. Now, if you and the lady will get back up

7

there and move along to the other side of the road block . . ."

"There was no road block when we came," said Wanda.

"There will be now, madam."

"Just a moment," said Masters. "I'm sure you have your reasons and your orders, but I'd like to know why my wife and I are being denied the use of a deserted public beach."

"Can't tell you that," said the constable, getting his wind back. "But I'd be on my way if I were you, mate. I don't want to stand here arguing with you all day."

"Careful," warned Masters, who was the last person on earth any constable should address as mate. Not only did Masters not like it for his own sake, but he was more than keen that policemen should show courtesy to the public at all times. He insisted on it among those who worked with him, and he expected it now. "I asked a reasonable question, and I expect a reasonable answer."

"Not from me," grunted the constable. "You can call at the station for your answers." He turned to Wanda. "Now, lady! Up you go." He put his hand out to turn her to face the wall.

Masters produced his wallet from the inside pocket of his parka with one hand, and with the other took a grip on the outstretched arm of the constable.

"I'll have you," grunted the uniformed man. "Assaulting a policeman in the . . ."

"Rubbish," grated Masters, allowing the wallet to fall open and display his warrant card. "Who is in charge of this operation?"

"George, please," said Wanda. "Don't cause a fuss."

They had been so immersed in their own situation that they had not noticed the approach of the sergeant along the promenade.

"What's going on here, Crowther?"

Masters looked up. "Are you in charge here, Sergeant?"

"Who wants to know?"

"I do."

"He's a . . . he's a Chief Superintendent, Sergeant."

"Oh! Well, sir."

"Well, sir, what?"

"Things on the beach," said the sergeant.

"Get down here and tell me what things," ordered Masters, who felt strongly disinclined to look up to the man standing above him.

The sergeant dropped heavily to the sand.

"Now? I want to know why you are interfering with the rights of the public without offering any explanation."

"Well, sir, there's been some heavy gales in the channel lately."

Masters nodded.

"One or two small coasters got into a bit of trouble and lost deck cargo. One actually sank."

Masters nodded again. He had read and heard of these incidents. Newspapers and news bulletins had been full of them.

"Well, sir, the breezes have been a bit fresh these last few days and setting inshore with the tide. Last night a number of things started to be washed up on the beach along here."

"What sort of things?"

"All sorts, sir. But what we're worried about are the chemicals."

"Canisters of chemicals?"

"That's right, sir. Arsenic something or another. I've got it written down." The sergeant took out his notebook, from which he took a folded sheet of paper.

"Arsenic trichloride, amino methyl propanol and phenyl benzanine," murmured Masters. "They sound dangerous."

"They are, sir. We've got everybody we can find looking for them and as many scientists as we can muster. We've even got the science master from the boys' school helping to handle them."

"Just the canisters?"

"That's right, sir. All the other bits and pieces that have been thrown up are being gathered by council workmen, but they've got strict orders not to touch unfamiliar objects."

"I see. Now, Sergeant, I'd like to give you a bit of advice."

"Yes, sir?"

"When you have to cause the general public some inconvenience, even in the line of serious duty, such as this, where you have to close the promenade and beach, for heaven's sake make sure that your men can offer some reasonable explanation."

"We were told not to mention the chemicals, sir."

"Why?"

"My inspector said we might cause alarm and despondency, sir."

"But that is monstrous, Sergeant. For two reasons. The first is that no matter how much you try to keep this operation quiet, every newshawk within two hundred miles will have it before teatime, and if they don't know the facts they'll make them up. The second is a more serious matter."

"Oh, yes, sir?"

"What if one of the dangerous canisters is washed up on a beach you haven't cordoned off? Some unsuspecting person may come across it and suffer because of the encounter. But if the public at large knows there are dangerous articles on the shore . . ."

"I get it, sir," said the sergeant. "I'll ask my inspector to change his mind and send a loud-speaker car round." He looked straight at Masters. "It would probably help, sir, if I were to have your name and say you had suggested it."

Masters grinned. "I understand, Sergeant. That's a polite way of asking to see my card for yourself." He again took out his wallet to display the warrant. As the sergeant inspected it, he asked: "I'd like your name in return."

"Gardam, sir."

"Thank you." As he put his wallet back into his pocket, Masters said to Crowther: "I don't like being called mate. Cure yourself of the habit, Constable."

He helped Wanda up on to the promenade and then followed her. Before they were out of earshot, they heard Gardam begin to berate Crowther. "Of all the bloody people on this floating island, Joe Crowther, you had to pick on that one to tangle with."

"I wasn't to know who he was, Sarge. I don't even know now, except he's a senior officer."

"Senior Officer? That's only George bloody Masters of Scotland bloody Yard. The bloke who's reckoned to be The Great-I-Am of all the jacks in the country."

"Oh!"

"Oh? Is that all you can say, Constable? You want to think yourself lucky he didn't lose his temper. I saw what was going on as

I came up. I reckon, Joe, that if you'd actually touched his missus—if he hadn't managed to stop you in time—he'd have put you in hospital. And serve you right! Mate, indeed!" The sergeant raised his eyes as if seeking assistance to help him believe it possible. "Calling Detective Chief Superintendent George Masters mate to his face and getting away with it! It must be your bloody birthday, Joe."

Arm in arm, Masters and Wanda strolled to the Jaguar—the one great luxury in their lives. "Where now, darling?"

"Cowes," replied Masters. "A stroll down the High Street there, looking at all the little shops, will be a change."

Masters drove across the island, through Newport. He was determined to make no comment as they passed Parkhurst prison. But Wanda, once she realised what it was, said: "I suppose quite a number of the guests are there at your invitation."

"I believe there are a few of my acquaintances inside. But not at my invitation. Most of them were positively insistent in proposing themselves for a stay."

"I'll take your word for it, but I don't think those in question would."

Masters didn't reply. He drove down into Cowes, parking the car in a side street to avoid the one-way system. Then, together, they worked their way down the narrow thoroughfare, crossing from side to side to gaze into the shops displaying boat fittings, antiques and sailing gear.

After coffee in a small café behind a confectioner's shop, they turned right down a narrow way to the sea-front to stroll along past the Royal Yacht Squadron and its battery of starting cannon. Wanda seemed blissfully happy, and Masters was more than content. The brush with Crowther was forgotten. Their last day on the island was as idyllic as they could have hoped. It was while they were making their way back to the little pub they had earmarked for lunch that they heard the police car patrolling the road and blaring out a warning to beware of unfamiliar objects on the beaches and to report suspicious items to the police or harbour authorities.

Chapter 2

WANDA'S BABY HAD been born. A son, Michael. He was a thriving, engaging scrap, and by the time he was three months old had a host of admirers. Not least among these were DCI Green and his wife, Doris. Though not yet ready to entrust her offspring to baby-sitters in the evenings, Wanda welcomed Doris Green's ever-ready offer to watch over Michael whilst she undertook the shopping expeditions necessary to keep herself and her family clothed and fed. When Mrs Green stood the afternoon watch, it was the understood thing that she should stay on, not only for a cup of tea, but to participate in the ceremony of bathing the baby—which started promptly at five-thirty—followed by feeding and snuggling down. By the time all this had been accomplished, it was mutually agreed that it would be too late for Doris to travel across London and then prepare supper for her husband who—at about the time the child normally closed its eyes to sleep—was customarily leaving the Yard at the end of the day's work. So Green would be instructed to walk home with Masters to the cottage behind Westminster Hospital to collect his wife or, more often, to stay for the evening meal.

It was on one such occasion—on an overcast day in July—that Masters and Green stopped to buy an evening paper just after crossing Victoria Street.

The double-deck headline was big and black: 'Botulism in West Country'. 'Family of Four in Danger'.

Masters glanced at it. Green read it over his shoulder. Masters folded the tabloid to carry as they continued on their way. "Rotten word, botulism," said the DCI. "Almost as bad as cancer."

"But not nearly so prevalent, thank heaven."

Green took a moment or two to reply, as though he were considering very carefully what he should say.

"Funny, though," he said at last.

"What is?"

"The incidence of botulism."

"Funny? Botulism?"

"The incidence. Not the disease itself."

"Sorry, Bill, I'm not following you."

"You said it is extremely rare in this country."

"Right."

"The last outbreak was in August seventy-eight, when those four people in Birmingham ate a contaminated tin of salmon."

"Even I can remember that," said Masters with a smile. Green had an encyclopaedic memory, and it was this which had, from time to time, lifted him out of the ordinary run of jacks and had allowed him to hold his own among the more imaginative men like Masters. *Experienta docet*, and experiences are only good teachers if you can remember them. Green remembered everything—just so long as it was given to him in simple English and not, to use his own words, in some fantouche lingo which, because he couldn't understand, he couldn't assimilate.

"I read an article about botulism when the Birmingham case was on," continued Green. "It said that the most serious outbreak ever in Britain was in nineteen twenty-two."

"Would that be the fishing party in Scotland?"

"At Loch Maree. Eight of them ate sandwiches made of potted duck and they all kicked the bucket."

"I remember reading about it—now you mention it."

"But do you remember that after that Loch Maree incident there were only two other cases in Britain before the Birmingham do? One in a macaroni café here in London a year or two after the war—forty-nine, I think it was—and the other in fifty-eight, caused by some pickled fish from Mauritius?"

"Go on. What's your point?"

"The intervals. Twenty-seven years between Loch Maree and the macaroni. Nine years between the macaroni and the Mauritian fish. Twenty years between the fish and Birmingham. And now, since Birmingham, less than two years to this business in the West Country."

"I see. That's the thing which strikes you as funny about the incidence?"

"Yes. The intervals should be lengthening, not shortening."

"Because of modern methods of food handling?" They stopped at the kerb to use the controlled crossing.

"That's why I said it was funny."

"I get your point. But surely, because botulism is so rare in this country, wouldn't you expect the intervals between outbreaks to be haphazard? Without any particular pattern?"

Green grunted—whether in assent or dissent was not apparent—but Masters was so accustomed to this particular form of equivocal acknowledgement that he ignored it and they continued in silence for the short distance that remained.

Green called it Wanda's palace, a name that suited the appointments but not the size of the little house. When he and Masters were in the tiny hall, they overcrowded it, particularly at this time when Master Michael Masters' perambulator was parked there.

Wanda appeared before they were fairly indoors. A shaft of early evening sun had broken through the clouds and had somehow found its way through the dining room window and into the little hall to silhouette her and shine through the gossamer strands of her very fine fair hair.

"Anything I can do?" asked Masters after he'd kissed her. "Lay the table or chop the mint?"

"All done. Doris is watching the vegetables and making the gravy." She turned to Green. "Hello, William. How are you?"

"Fair-to-middlin'," replied Green with a grin. "We've got a lot in common, you know, love. We both have to suffer His Nibs here."

"Has he been getting you down?"

"He's been behaving fairly well recently. I'll let you into a secret. I don't think he's been really with us since the sprog came along."

"I knew he was very happy with his son, but I didn't know it was affecting his work."

"Something terrible. But how is the boyo? Can I creep up and take a peep at him?"

"Don't be long. We'll be ready for you in ten minutes."

"Make it a quarter of an hour," pleaded Masters. "Then Bill and I can have a drink when we get down."

They were all four in the sitting room—a crowd for so small a room—when Green put down his drink and asked: "Could we have the mid-evening news?"

"Bill!" expostulated his wife. "You don't ask for the telly in other people's houses."

"I have done, love."

"I'd like to hear the news myself," said Masters, switching on. "The evening paper says there's been an outbreak of botulism."

"Where?"

"In the west country, somewhere. I've not had time to read the article."

"Oh dear," said Wanda. "That does make me nervous. I shall be putting Michael on tinned baby foods, and . . ."

"You've nothing to worry about," said Doris Green firmly. "You're feeding him yourself and there's months to go before he's on tinned food."

"Good idea, feeding him yourself," added her husband. "Natural. Gives him all the protection in the world and saves him from allergies in later life."

"You seem to know all about it," said Masters with a grin.

"Read it up, Doris and me, as soon as we knew Wanda was expecting."

"You did what?"

"Read it up. Ah! This is it. Let's have a bit of sound on that contraption, George."

The announcer's voice filled the room.

". . . outbreak of botulism on Exmoor. Four people, Mr and Mrs Burnham and their two young children, aged ten and eight, are in hospital in Taunton. The Burnham family are believed to have eaten a tin of ham for their tea three evenings ago. The four were taking a camping holiday on Exmoor and were catering for themselves. Doctors at the Taunton and Somerset Hospital have issued a statement about the family's condition. It says that all four are seriously ill, their condition having been aggravated by the fact that because they had chosen an isolated spot for their camp, no medical help had been given until thirty-six hours after the suspected ham had been eaten. Two students on a walking tour discovered the four Burnhams lying in and around their tent, and after realising they were ill, had to summon help. Here is our medical correspondent, Oliver Garside."

The image of the newsreader disappeared and the features of a full-fleshed man took its place. The newcomer spoke in the racy, pseudo-knowledgeable way of one who, though not thoroughly informed on the subject has, nevertheless, boned up on it just enough to half-inform the lay listener.

"Botulism! The name comes from the Latin, botulus, meaning a sausage and refers to the fact that in the old days, before canning and preserving, most outbreaks of the disease resulted from eating contaminated sausages. Clostridium botulinum, to give it its full medical name, is a dangerous bacterium. Dangerous because it is poisons given off by the bacteria, known as exotoxins, which cause anybody unfortunate enough to ingest them to become seriously ill. The disease is almost invariably the result of eating imperfectly canned or bottled meats or fish, and the fatality rate in humans is usually at least fifty per cent and often higher.

"The Burnham family is thought to have eaten a commercially canned ham at about six o'clock, three evenings ago. The symptoms of botulism are not like those of ordinary food-poisoning in that there is rarely—if ever—any diarrhoea. There is, however, vomiting, though the most serious symptoms are the result of the poison affecting the nervous system—particularly the nerves of the eyes and the throat, which are paralysed. These symptoms begin between twelve and thirty-six hours after eating contaminated food. So what probably happened in the case of the Burnhams was that the whole family went to bed three nights ago apparently fit and well. But the next morning—at any time after six o'clock—they could have all been feeling extremely ill. Too ill, perhaps, to summon help.

"It is highly probable that Mr Burnham, the one whom one might have expected to attempt to get help for his family, was, in fact, the most seriously ill. Being a grown man he probably ate

16

much more of the affected food than did his wife or young children, and the point about botulism is that the more one ingests of it, the more dangerous the symptoms are liable to be. Mr Burnham was, therefore, probably the most intoxicated of the four—because intoxication is what botulism is—intoxication caused by exotoxins.

"Their plight would gradually grow worse and their condition, when discovered by the two students who summoned medical help at lunchtime yesterday would, I am reliably informed, be extremely grave, because survival depends so much on prompt treatment. And one must remember that before the disease can be correctly diagnosed, long and difficult tests must be made."

The face of the newsreader reappeared to continue the bulletin.

"If that's all you want to see," said Wanda, "everything is ready for supper."

The dining-room was bigger. Long for its width, it ran right across the back of the cottage and had given Wanda the opportunity and space to plan the room she wanted. It was here—if anywhere—that was apparent the good taste that had caused Green to christen the place Wanda's little palace. He loved the room and, apparently, the meals served in it.

"Proper lamb that," he said appreciatively.

"Of course it's proper lamb," retorted his wife.

"I know what William means," said Wanda. "He'd like some more. George!" She handed the empty plate to her husband, who immediately started to carve more meat for his colleague.

"Actually," said Green, eyeing Masters' carving appreciatively, "I meant what I said. When I was a lad, there was such a thing as mutton. Saddle of mutton, mutton chops, mutton ham . . ."

"Mutton ham?"

"A leg of mutton cured like a pork ham. Very good, too. They tried to make bacon the same way during the war. Macon they called it, but it didn't catch on. But in those days we used to eat onion sauce with mutton and mint sauce with lamb. Now every blessed bit of sheep meat, old or young, is lamb."

"I agree with you," said Masters, passing Green the replenished plate. "When I was a boy we used to eat beef pie. Now it's all steak pie."

"Do you know my pet hate," said Doris Green, helping her husband from the tureens. "I'm not a woman anymore. I'm a lady. All those TV chat-show people have decided it's wrong to use an honest-to-goodness word like woman."

"That's ladies' lib for you," said her husband, spooning mint sauce on to his meat. "I always thought women's lib was bad enough, but ladies' lib . . ." He grimaced and attacked his food.

When the meal was over, the two men offered to wash up. Masters had taken his jacket off and donned a plastic apron emblazoned with a Real Ale campaign ad while Green had the tea towel at the ready when Wanda came through to the kitchen.

"Darling!"

"Yes, poppet?" Masters was washing his glasses in plain warm water. He refused to use soap or washing-up liquid for them.

"There's been another outbreak of botulism, they think."

"Think?"

"Doris and I had the ten o'clock news on. Reports are just coming in about the suspected outbreak. They say it's somewhere in Essex."

"Anything else, love?" asked Green.

"I'm afraid so. The younger of the two children in Taunton has died."

"Poor little kid," said Green quietly. "It makes you wonder, doesn't it?"

"We'll be through before the end of the news," said Masters. "There may be some more details then."

Wanda left them and the two men continued with their chores. As Green folded the teacloth and hung it over the towel rail, he said: "I suppose the people in Essex bought a tin of ham from the same batch as the Burnhams."

"That would seem to be the most likely thing to have happened," agreed Masters, putting on his jacket. "But I'm surprised they haven't announced the batch number and warned people to be on the look-out for it."

"They daren't," said Green, feeling in his pockets for cigarettes and matches. "Not yet. That tin of ham is only suspected. The report said the Burnhams had *apparently* eaten it, are *believed* to have eaten it, and so on. Anybody who comes straight out and says it was definitely the cause of the trouble—before the doctors and scientists have proved it—could be liable."

Masters nodded. "Still, there should be some means of early warning—without prejudice—to alert people. I mean, they wouldn't even have to name the brand. They could issue a blanket request not to eat any form of tinned ham until the matter was settled one way or another."

The two men went through to the sitting room.

"Nothing more about the Essex outbreak," said Wanda, "so we switched off because I want to talk to William."

"Lovely," said Green. "Here? Or shall we go where we can be alone?"

"Silly ass!" said his wife. "She'd be as safe alone with you as she would be on a desert island."

"Spoilsport!" laughed Wanda. She turned to Green. "Our elder, unmarried son . . ."

"You've only got one and he's only about three months old."

"You never know. We may have another, and he'll come unmarried, too."

"I wouldn't be too sure. There was a young lass went back to school at some Comprehensive after her honeymoon the other day. White knee-socks and a gymslip . . ."

"Be quiet," ordered Doris. "Wanda wants to say something."

"Brandy, Bill?" asked Masters.

"I'm not allowed to say," whispered Green, "but if you were to shove one in my mitt I couldn't say no."

"Our son," resumed Wanda, "is shortly to be christened. He, being a boy, needs by tradition, two godfathers and one godmother. As we propose to give him the same name as you, William, will you consent to be one of his godparents?"

Green did not reply immediately. In the silence they all watched his face. Incredulity and delight struggled for possession of his round, heavy features.

"Oh, Bill!" breathed his wife.

"Give him my name? But he's already called Michael."

"Michael William Masters," said Wanda with a smile. "Doesn't that sound strong and fine?"

Green looked enquiringly at Masters who said, "We both wanted you, Bill. Unanimous decision with no discussion necessary."

Green set down the brandy glass Masters had handed him. "I don't have to tell you, do I? I never dreamed . . . godfather to the young sprog! Me!"

"Well!" asked his wife.

"The pleasure," said Green handsomely, "will be entirely mine."

Wanda rose and kissed him. "Thank you, William."

"My cousin and his wife will be your partners in crime, Bill," said Masters. "Like you, they have no children of their own and are delighted to . . ."

The sound of the phone bell cut through his words. Wanda went out to the tiny hall to answer it. She was back very quickly.

"It's Edwin Anderson, darling," she said quietly.

"Ringing from home?"

"From the office."

Masters got to his feet. Green said, "What in the name of all that's holy is the AC Crime doing at the Yard at this time of night? He should be at home doing his pools or playing Mah Jong."

"Bridge," corrected Wanda absent-mindedly. "He plays bridge. Rather badly, actually."

Her tone caused Green to glance across at her. "Cheer up, love. It's only another job for George."

"I know, William. It's just that being this late at night it must be an important call. And important calls usually mean that you two are going to be away for days on end."

"I warned you," grinned Green. "I told you not to marry a copper, but you would have your own way."

"You're a liar, Bill Green," said his wife. "You encouraged them."

"I had to marry George," said Wanda, "just so I could stay in touch with you, William. If I hadn't joined the Yard I might never have seen you again."

Green beamed at her. Doris said: "You wouldn't have said that if you'd been married to him for thirty years."

The DCI got no chance to reply. Masters came into the room looking grave. "We're wanted, Bill."

"What, now?"

Wanda smiled tremulously at her husband, who sensed the question in her mind.

"It's this botulism affair, darling."

"Why you? I thought the local health authorities would deal with that?"

"And the police," grunted Green. "They're always involved in the tracking down of suspect food."

"But surely not the CID from Scotland Yard?"

"I must agree it seems a bit unusual, but if the outbreaks could be widespread they might want us to co-ordinate the local forces."

Wanda shook her head. "No good, William. It's more serious than that, isn't it George?"

"Can you tell us?" asked Doris Green.

Masters said: "The second outbreak is now confirmed. It was caused not by a tin of ham, but by a tin of canned beef."

"They're positive?" asked Green.

"As sure as they can be at the moment."

Green said quietly. "That's bad. But I'd guess from your attitude that there's more to come, George."

Wanda exclaimed, "Oh, no!"

Masters nodded. "A third suspected outbreak in Derby. But this time it's a tin of luncheon meat."

Wanda went to her husband. "What does it mean, George?"

"It means, my precious, that there's something terribly wrong somewhere, and they want Bill and me to find out what."

Green got to his feet. "Then the sooner we get weaving, the better, George." He turned to his wife. "Ring for a taxi, love."

"Doris will stay here tonight," said Wanda firmly. "The spare bed is made up and she can't go home alone to an empty house at this time of night."

*

"This," said Anderson angrily, "is going to be a bastard, George. Epidemics and what-have-you are not our business."

"In that case, sir, why is Crime involved and not Administration or Uniform?"

They were sitting in Anderson's office waiting for three others who were to attend the conference. A trolley with coffee and sandwiches had been brought in together with the extra chairs.

"The Home Office," grunted Anderson, in reply to Masters' question. "They want us in."

"To co-ordinate the local police activities, sir?"

"Their advisers say there's something fishy about the whole business, George."

"By that you mean criminal?"

"So they say."

"Reasons for saying so?" asked Green.

"First of all, incidence," replied Anderson. Green smirked. He had made the same point earlier. "There reckons to be a decade or two between isolated outbreaks of botulism in the U.K. It's barely two years since the Birmingham case. Second, they would not have been so worried if the three outbreaks we know about had been caused by the same type of food from the same batch or from the same manufacturer. But there are three foods involved—ham from Denmark, bully beef from South America and meat loaf from Holland. All at once. They can't swallow the coincidence. And neither will the public."

"They believe that these foods have been contaminated for a purpose, sir? It seems unbelievable. For what reason?"

"That's where we come in—or rather, you do. Somehow we've got to contain a panic . . ."

"There won't be one," muttered Green.

"Maybe not if there are no more outbreaks," replied Anderson. "But what if there are two more tomorrow and three the day after? And that seems a distinct possibility to me if the contamination has been criminally induced and the perpetrator has made a thorough job of it."

Green nodded to show he appreciated the logic of this possibility and proceeded to ask the AC if the public was to be warned against using the foods he had mentioned.

Anderson spread his hands. "We warn them against three types of food, and then there's a fourth outbreak implicating a tin of herrings in tomato sauce. Then how do we stand?"

"Nevertheless, sir," said Masters, "there should be some warning given."

"Against all tinned foods? The country would starve. Think of supermarkets, George. Nothing but tins. Think of late-night shoppers with those damned trolleys piled high with nothing but tins." Anderson expired. "Green says there'd be no panic. There'd be bloody food riots!"

While his subordinates were digesting this rather unpalatable morsel of clairvoyance, there was a knock at the door, and a uniformed constable ushered in three men. Anderson got to his feet to make the introductions.

The newcomers were Chief Superintendent Wigglesworth, the Home Office Police Co-ordinator; Professor Convamore the eminent pathologist; and Dr Moller, a Principal Scientific Officer from the government forensic department.

Anderson poured the coffee and spoke as he did so. "As I see it, gentlemen, Scotland Yard will take responsibility for any criminal aspects of this business. But nothing more. The local health and safety authorities can deal with their individual medical problems. They've got the expertise and the staffs to do it, whereas I don't suppose we even know how to spell . . . what is it? . . . clostridium botulinum. As it is, I've assigned Masters and Green to the investigation—as being the most knowledgeable about medical matters among my senior staff."

"The best pair you could give us, sir," said Wigglesworth. Convamore, who had worked with Masters on several previous occasions, winked at him surreptitiously, as much as to say that he agreed with Wigglesworth but regretted the Co-ordinator's unctuous way of putting it.

When he was again seated at his desk, Anderson said: "I'll try to paint the overall picture—what little I know of it. You gentlemen can then make what contributions you like in a general discussion."

23

"We can interrupt to ask questions, sir?"

"For clarification, George, certainly. But I don't want to be here till dawn."

"Thank you, sir."

The AC began. "There have been three almost simultaneous but widespread outbreaks of botulism. One in Somerset confirmed; one in Essex virtually certain; and one in Derby suspected. The first two have been announced in news bulletins, the third is being kept quiet for as long as possible for two reasons. The first so that the diagnosis can be fully confirmed. The second to try and dampen down the public dismay—if not panic—that an impression of widespread botulism could cause."

"There could be more incidents," reminded Wigglesworth.

"If so," replied Anderson, "I would expect the Director of the Communicable Diseases Surveillance Centre to know as soon as there are any more suspected cases."

"Not quite right, Edwin," asserted Convamore. "No doctor is going to want to start hares of that sort. He may suspect botulism—among other things—but he's going to be pretty sure in his own mind before he sounds the alarm."

"And this suspected case in Derby?"

"They'll be sure of it," said the pathologist. "Sure of it in the patients, that is, though they may not have completed their tests to isolate the peccant food."

"Is that really so?"

"It has to be. There are too many variables for any diagnosis to be anything like definite without tests. So by the time a doctor says he suspects botulism, he's a long way down the road to proving it."

"That suggests there is a hideous time lag," said Anderson.

"Let me explain. You just said you would expect the Director of the Communicable Diseases Surveillance Centre to be alerted at the first signs. He won't be so alerted."

"No? Why not?"

"Because botulism—as such—is not a notifiable disease."

"It's not?" queried Green, astounded by such a revelation from such an authority as the Professor.

24

"Not in its own right, though it may come to be notified as food poisoning. It is quite simple, gentlemen. The notifiable diseases are cholera, plague, relapsing fever, smallpox, typhus and food poisoning—all diseases which spread. Botulism is—or may be—regarded as a form of food poisoning, but it doesn't spread from person to person and so is non-communicable. But remember that food poisoning is difficult to define. The most common form is acute enteritis and so, through common usage, it—that is food poisoning—is now accepted as meaning gastroenteritis following the consumption of unwholesome food or drink. And so we do not include specific infectious diseases like enteric fever in this category, even though they are often spread by infected drinking water." He looked round and said, parenthetically, "When I said often, in this context, I do not mean that outbreaks of enteric fever are common in this country. Indeed, they are extremely rare. But where and when they do occur elsewhere in the world, contaminated water is frequently the cause."

"Thank heaven for that bit of reassurance," said Anderson gloomily.

Convamore continued.

"Nor does one include as notifiable food poisoning illness due to a food idiosyncrasy or food allergy, since the food that has been eaten in such cases is wholesome—like shellfish—and it is the patient's reaction to it that is abnormal. There are other categories, too. Food that is too rich, like fat and cream, and food that is mechanically irritating, like unripe apples. All these can cause apparent food poisoning. So, gentlemen, the doctor who first sees a case may, to begin with, consider he has not met one of the complaints he is obliged to notify. And I would add that he may well be misled by botulism, because the chances are thousands to one against him having encountered it previously. Furthermore, he may not even suspect that the trouble has anything to do with food because food poisoning, classically, causes diarrhoea, whereas botulism does not."

"Never?" asked Anderson.

"The answer to that," retorted Convamore, "is a lemon."

"You mean there could be exceptions to the rule?"

25

"Precisely. And not always due to the botulinum bug, either. So often people have minor tummy upsets which do give them the trots. Give them a dose of botulism on top of that and it could be totally misleading because, one would imagine, another severe disease of the stomach could well exacerbate one already there." Convamore gestured with both hands. "All in all gentlemen, botulism is often far from easy to suspect, let alone confirm."

"You're warning us to expect more cases," said Anderson glumly.

"All I am saying is that it would be unsafe to assume there are no more to come."

"Not much difference," grunted Green.

"And just one more thing, Assistant Commissioner." Convamore leaned forward to make his point. "It is the duty of the doctor examining the patient to furnish the Community Physician for the district with the details of the communicable disease or the poisoning the patient is, or is suspected to be, suffering from. Community physicians are doctors, but by reason of the posts they hold, they are also part-bureaucrats. So you can imagine that, before they start spreading alarm and despondency, they're going to want to be doubly sure that the diagnosis is pretty certain. I only add this bit of information to let you know that there could be a slight bureaucratic hesitation before a case is openly declared to be botulism."

"Christmas night!" growled Green. "It's a wonder we ever get anywhere with this sort of thing."

"I'd like to get on," said Anderson querulously, thereby rebuking Green for his remark. "Specifically I want to explain to Masters and Green why they should have been called in on a case that is ostensibly the responsibility of the local health authorities concerned—with the aid of local police if needs be."

"The Yard," said Wigglesworth plummily, "is at the disposal of any police force, world-wide, should its services be required."

"Not required," snapped Anderson. "Requested."

"Quite," said Wigglesworth. "The Home Office, as the supreme police authority in the country has—er—requested the help of the Yard. No Yard involvement would have been contemplated had all three attacks of botulism followed the ingestion of one single type of food. Had all the victims eaten, say, tinned ham, it would have been assumed either that one complete batch of ham was infected or that the canning factory involved was to blame and that all its output would be suspect. But as you already know, there are three different foods involved, made by three different manufacturers in three different countries. That is the reason for our suspicion of criminal involvement."

"Also," said Anderson heavily, "there is the fact that all three infected tins came from the same chain of stores. Different branches, perhaps, but the same chain."

"Ah!" said Masters. "We hadn't heard that."

"Redcoke Stores," said Wigglesworth.

"My missus shops there," said Green.

"And mine," added Anderson. "Which woman doesn't? And that highlights our problem, George. If there are any other outbreaks—from different foodstuffs—we should have to close down every Redcoke branch, and that's the equivalent of shutting almost half the grocery outlets in the country."

"Not only that," said Moller. "Most housewives will have a few tins of Redcoke products on their shelves. My wife uses their tinned carrots among other things. I mention carrots because we eat a lot of them and we always have half a dozen tins in hand. Botulism, as you probably know, is not confined to fish and meat. It goes for vegetables, too, particularly those in close contact with the soil. In fact, I think I'm right in saying that there are several outbreaks every year in the States due to imperfectly preserved vegetables. They do a lot of domestic bottling and canning there, of course, whereas there is very little done in this country. My point is, if three Redcoke lines have already caused botulism, with the likely prospect of more to come, scores of millions of pounds' worth of probably wholesome food will be ditched in panic."

"A costly business for the country," observed Convamore. "One the nation cannot afford, let alone individual citizens."

"Heaven only knows what it will do to the Redcoke trade."

"It could mean complete closure for them, George."

"And another few thousand unemployed," grunted Green.

27

"Quite. So we appreciate how important it is for us, the police, to discover how their goods are becoming infected and then how to stop it happening. The various health authorities, meanwhile, will deal with the medical problems. Does that look like a fair division of labour, gentlemen?"

Green sniffed, as if to imply that Anderson was suggesting the impossible. "We don't even know for sure that there has been criminal activity," he said. He looked across at Moller. "Isn't it up to the Horseferry House boys to examine everything, backwards down the line to stops and then to call George and myself in if they reckon they need us?"

Anderson looked across at Moller for his reaction to this suggestion. The scientist replied: "The Forensic Science Service will do exactly what Mr Green has outlined—as far as we can. In fact, our people are already on the way to collect the three tins for examination and comparison."

"Comparison?"

"There are several types of botulism," murmured Convamore. "Just to complicate things."

Moller continued. "We must know whether the same type is implicated in all the outbreaks. If they are not all the same . . ." He shrugged. "If there are two different types implicated, we've come up against a million to one chance—at a conservative estimate. If there are three types, the chances are scores of millions to one. But we shall test all three tins here, in our own laboratory—and keep our fingers crossed. Then, Mr Green, depending on what we find, we shall work backwards just as you suggested. But going back to stops, as you put it, will be easier said than done because each of the products, as you already know, originates in a different foreign country."

"International difficulties," said Wigglesworth. "The Ministry will want to avoid those."

"Exactly," said Moller. "So, Mr Green, as I believe coincidences or longodds or whatever you like to call them are an occupational hazard of your everyday police work, whereas we forensic scientists only state what we actually see under our microscopes, we shall need your help from the outset."

"Fair enough," said Green. "What you're saying is that three outbreaks at once almost certainly suggests hanky panky. If there were three different types of botulism implicated, it would be certain."

"Precisely."

"The international implications . . ." began Wigglesworth.

"There won't be any," said Masters quietly. "Not unless we make unfounded accusations or wild guesses. And I feel sure that each of the producing countries would co-operate with us willingly, either to preserve their own good names or in the interests of world health—should the need arise. You may assure the Ministry that any investigation carried out by Green and myself will be done diplomatically."

Having dealt with Wigglesworth, Masters turned to Anderson. "I think, sir, as the question of diplomacy—and with it, of necessity, the business of public information—has now arisen, that we should decide on a single spokesman, so that we shall not all make statements which could be contradictory and, because of that, could give rise to more mischievous speculation than might otherwise be the case."

"I take your point, George. We can't muzzle the reporters but we must be firm and single-minded in what we say." He turned to the Co-ordinator. "What about you, Mr Wigglesworth? You would represent the Home Office as well as the Police."

"No, no, no," objected Convamore. "The Chief Super doesn't know enough about the disease and its implications."

"Well . . ." began Wigglesworth, a wealth of affront in his tone.

"We want a boffin to do it," continued the Professor paying no heed to the hurt he had done the Co-ordinator. "A boffin won't be blinded by science from some of these sassy young inquisitors from the media—so called."

"Whom do you suggest? Yourself?"

"Not me. Moller. He's an investigative scientist and he'll be in charge of that side of our affairs."

"I second that, sir," said Masters. "As yet, Green and I have no specific lines of investigation. Dr Moller is already involved. Besides, his techniques—experiments and such—make much more

29

interesting copy than the routine stuff the Professor and we shall be doing."

"Hear, hear," said Convamore.

Anderson nodded his agreement.

"In that case," said Moller, "I'll deal with all press matters if you others promise to arrange for all queries to be directed to Dean Ryle Street."

"The Computer Unit and all the others in Horseferry House won't like it," counselled Green. "Scads of reporters and TV cameras cluttering the place up."

"They'll have to like it or lump it," said Moller. "I can see myself incarcerated in my office for days, if not weeks, over this little party. And if I can't get out to go home, I'm certainly not getting out to answer questions."

"That's the ticket," said Convamore approvingly. "This show is going to be a big enough headache without the sensation-mongers cashing in. The last time those boyos interviewed me they cut me down to less than two minutes. Left me dangling in mid-air like a nit-wit who hadn't let go of his kite."

"I remember it," said Green. "It was the only academic interview I've ever heard that ended with the word arse."

Convamore laughed. "Actually, I said arsenic, but they cut me off between syllables."

"Gentlemen," said Anderson tetchily, "can we please get on?"

"What else is there to discuss?" asked Convamore. "I shall look after the pathology, Moller will tackle the technical side, while Masters and Green do their stuff, drawing information from both of us as well as from their own investigations."

"Botulism itself, Professor," said Masters. "Green and I must know something about it."

"For background? Of course."

"In understandable terms," added Green.

"Well now . . . where to begin . . .?"

"Perhaps it would help," cut in Masters, "if we were to know how botulism gets into tins. Every day we blithely eat tinned food without giving botulism a thought. We rely on the fact that rotten food will blow a tin, and so we avoid using damaged or distended cans. Why haven't the contaminated tins shown themselves up in this way?"

"I get your line of thought," said Convamore. "I'll try to explain in simple terms. Moller, perhaps you would chip in if you think of anything I may miss."

"With pleasure."

"Remember please," said Masters, "that with no real evidence to help us, Green and I have been asked to presume the probability of crime. If we are to confirm its presence and then run it to earth, we must understand what we are dealing with. So, though we want an explanation in terms a child would understand, we must have every detail."

Convamore nodded his understanding. He was a big man, but already showing the signs of natural shrinkage that comes with age. His head was almost completely bald: the close-cropped fringe that remained was grey. His broad shoulders had an academic stoop—a roundness emphasised by the thinness of the material of his fawn jacket which embodied none of the usual tailor's padding or stiffening. Yet he was fully alert and showing no signs of fatigue despite the hour. He struck Masters—who had worked with him on several previous occasions—as a man who enjoyed work and drew his energy and enthusiasm from participation in the job. Even a matter so serious as three simultaneous outbreaks of botulism seemed to cause him pleasure: not pleasure at the events themselves, but delight at being required to deal with them once they had occurred.

Moller, though not cast in the same physical mould, appeared to be reacting in exactly the same way as Convamore. The repercussions and dangers were seemingly forgotten in the enthusiasm for tackling the job with which he was now faced.

Masters could understand Moller's attitude. Some time previously, he, Masters, had endured a conducted tour of the forensic laboratory. The scientist who had accompanied him had been justly proud of what he had to show and describe. Much of it had been above Masters' head, but he had remembered something of what he had been told. The number of tests that could be—and were—carried out to determine the identity of even the minutest specks of suspect substances. The benches on which the painstakingly detailed work was done. The equipment—melting point apparatus, polarimeter, refractometer, spectrophotometer infra-red spectrophotometer, photoelectric colorimeter, and chromotography apparatus—just a few of the items he had remembered. And the tests themselves: for the separation of poisons, for reactions with reagents with names some of which were familiar, others not—benzedine-copper acetate, Prussian blue, silver nitrate, ethyl acetate and a hundred more. Tests named after the scientists who had introduced them—Leibig, Schilt, Cole, Rozeboom, Sawicki and Stanley and so on and so on.

Masters wanted none of this. He and Green would simply founder—not just blinded by science, but drowned by it. He felt he had to make certain from the outset that the differing enthusiasms of the pathologist and forensic scientist should not be allowed to fog his own investigation. So he repeated his injunction to the two scientists: "Every detail, please, gentlemen, but in lay terms."

"Right." It was Convamore who started off. "There are two difficult words which you must know if we're to understand each other. The first is *proteolytic*. A proteolytic organism is one which causes food to decompose and to smell bad."

"Are any of the botulism types proteolytic?" asked Masters.

"Yes, praise be! It helps us to isolate the type that's causing the trouble. Types A, B and E are the ones which usually cause human disease. But of these, types A and B produce gas which causes blown tins. They are proteolytic."

"So," said Green, to show he was taking it all in, "unless the three lots of people who ate the contaminated food were all blind and had no sense of smell, the botulism we are looking for is type E."

"Correct—so far as we can say at the moment, but while concentrating on type E, keep an open mind—just in case."

"That's a great help," said Masters. "Elimination of alternatives is always good."

"Not this time," said Moller. "Or rather, I should say, it could well be a complication."

"Why?"

32

"Because," said Moller, "types A and B are those usually found in Britain. Type E is extremely rare here."

"I knew it," said Green glumly. "We're on a needle-in-a-haystack job. We've now got to look for a source of trouble that doesn't exist in this country."

"It looks a bit like that, I'm afraid."

Anderson got up to pass the plate of sandwiches round. His face and manner showed that he was as pessimistic as Green had sounded.

"Extremely rare?" asked Masters. "Could scarcity be a help to us rather than a hindrance?"

"I reckon not," said Moller, talking through a mouthful of sandwich. "Types A and B are rife in Britain . . ."

"Rife?"

"Everywhere in the soil. The bacteria themselves, that is. But the bacteria are harmless to humans. It's the exotoxins they produce under ideal conditions that do the damage. The clostridia produces a spore—like a vegetable produces a seed—and this vegetative growth produces the poison—known as an exotoxin—but only, I repeat, under suitable conditions."

"And type E?"

"Is so rare that I think it must be spread very thinly everywhere rather than being in great numbers in just a few spots. So its rarity factor is unlikely to help your search."

"I understand—and I'm rather frightened."

"Aren't we all?" said Convamore. "Now for the second word you must understand. It is *anaerobic*."

"Meaning without air?" asked Masters.

"Without oxygen, actually. Botulism spores are totally anaerobic. They will not tolerate any oxygen. So, before they can thrive and produce their exotoxins, they need a can or jar of food from which all air has been dispelled. That is why they are not normally dangerous in body cells—we have oxygen in all areas of the body."

"They are kept quiescent if there is air about," said Masters. "But what kills them totally? Heat?"

"Just so. Food manufacturers sterilise all canned and bottled foods at a high heat for a long time. That is why botulism is so very rare."

"What you've said doesn't make sense," growled Green. "If the spores in those tins of meat had been killed off by heat, how could they come to life again?"

"Spores must have got into the tins after the heating process."

"They couldn't. The tins are sealed before heating."

"Perhaps a small hole . . ." suggested Wigglesworth.

"No," said Green emphatically, "because if there was a small hole to let the spores in, it would let the air in, too. And the little swine won't reproduce if there's air about."

"And that," said Convamore, "is the problem you have to solve, Mr Green.

"Thanks."

Anderson roused himself. "Any more questions, George?"

"Yes, sir. I want to return to the incidence of type E. Is it common, for instance, in South America where the bully-beef came from?"

"I know we are all liable to presume that the South American countries are more infested with nasties than we are," said Convamore, "but in this case we should be wrong to do so. Type E is not found in southern latitudes."

"Northern hemisphere only?"

"Virtually. And although it is common, for instance, in northern Canada and Alaska, it is comparatively rare here. It may be common, for all I know, in Siberia, too, but that's as much as I can tell you."

Anderson looked across at Convamore. "Is that it, Professor?"

"Just one last point, Edwin. Just in case our friends haven't realised it yet, I think I should emphasise that the botulinum exotoxin is one of the most powerful—if not the most powerful—of known poisons. It is hard to say what is the lethal dose for a man, but it is generally accepted as being a ten millionth of a gramme. And a gramme is a mighty small amount. It is also generally accepted as being twenty-five times as deadly as the tetanus toxin. So the watchword, should you come up against the enemy in the flesh, as it were, is 'handle with care', gentlemen."

Chapter 3

"I FEEL," SAID Green as he and Masters stepped into the open air and the morning twilight, "as if that meeting was nothing but a bad dream from which I haven't yet wakened up."

"It's the time of day," replied Masters. "Gone four o'clock. No sleep and ears bashed with scientific facts."

"Not that," said Green. "I could have taken that and just been bored with it. It's what might happen, George, if you don't stop it."

"We," corrected Masters.

"I said you and I meant you." Green sounded weary. "I honestly haven't a clue as to how to start. If it's left to me we'll not make a move."

"You're tired. Come on, step out, and you can have a few hours' kip at the cottage. Get undressed and climb in beside Doris and you'll be snoring away in no time. We won't have breakfast till nine o'clock."

"Won't you want to be out on the job early?"

"The answer to that is yes. But quite honestly, like you, I don't know where to begin. Furthermore, I shall not be in a position to decide what I want to do until I'm fresh and can think straight."

"You can always think straight—tired or otherwise."

"In normal cases, perhaps. But not with a problem as complex as this. You see, Bill, I can't forget that most pertinent point you made?"

"Which one?" asked Green, as though he had spent the entire night making pertinent points.

"When you said that botulism could not enter a tin through a hole without letting air in at the same time, thereby not allowing the anaerobic spores to grow."

35

Green shrugged. His brain was obviously too tired for comment.

Masters continued. "That's illogical. To solve the illogical, one has to be bright and fresh. Then there's the big problem not one of us mentioned."

"What?" asked Green.

"If a man put the botulism into those tins, where did he get the botulism from?"

"Cripes!" said Green, waking up a little. "He'd have to . . . what's the word? . . . culture it?"

"Precisely," said Masters taking the front door key from his pocket. "And that's enough for tonight. We'll carry on after breakfast."

"Where on earth are you going to start, darling?"

"Now, love," said Green, accepting the plate of bacon and eggs from Wanda, "don't start him off. I said much the same thing to your old man as we left the Yard this morning. Before we got as far as your front door he'd explained to me—and I was bushed at the time so you can tell how straight he must have been talking for me to take it in—he'd explained that we are looking for a chemist of pretty good standing . . ."

"Why?"

"Because only a clever geezer in that line could culture the stuff in the first place."

"That's good thinking."

"I said so, didn't I? And the clever scientist has to be a clever technician."

"Has he?"

"He's got to be more than that. He's got to be a magician. One who can wave a wand and send dollops of botulism bugs into a can of meat without puncturing the skin."

"Good heavens! That's impossible," said his wife.

"Right," said Green, savaging an egg. 'Bloody impossible and we've got to sort it." He filled his mouth and turned to Wanda. "So I'm opting out, love, and leaving it to His Nibs."

"That would be a great pity," replied Wanda seriously, "because millions of people will be relying on you to save their lives or

36

at least to remove the threat of death. They won't know it's you, of course. Just that a few men, whom they trust implicitly, are working away on their behalf. I know I'm relying on you, and George, and Sergeant Reed and Sergeant Berger. And so is Michael—although he doesn't know it."

Green had stopped eating and was staring at her.

"That's how you really look at it, isn't it, love?"

"Yes, it is."

Green shook his head. "I'm out of my depth with this one. Oh, I know I can't back out. But I really do feel helpless."

Wanda smiled. "Just like Doris and me, Bill, but we have faith in you. Please try your hardest—as I know you will—to see that too many people don't die."

Green turned to the silent Masters. "Is that the sort of approach she usually makes? Because if so, she must get her own way all the time."

Masters nodded. "She's very wise, Bill."

Green picked up his cup. "I wonder if she's been wise enough to brew enough coffee to refill this for me?"

Detective Sergeants Reed and Berger listened to the briefing given them by Masters in his office and—to his dismay—adopted almost the same attitude as that previously taken by Green. They viewed the investigation as something beyond their capabilities. They were, Masters guessed, frightened by the word botulism and its attendant danger to life. The technical side of the enquiry—or thoughts of it—also bemused them. Normally tolerant of obtuseness or the odd mental blockage in his assistants, Master was not prepared to accept a defeatist attitude at the outset of a case of this importance. To their great surprise—because they had never before been subjected to such treatment—he roasted them verbally. They sat, red-faced and amazed while he spelled out to them—forcefully—that a detective's training, and indeed his whole life in the force, were, in essence, only a preparation for the big and difficult case. Catching a murderer who had killed once and was unlikely to repeat his crime was important, but nowhere near as important as protecting the whole populace from a pathological fiend who appeared intent on widespread slaughter without thought or reason. They—Reed and Berger—would, therefore, stop enumerating the difficulties, and get down to work, physically and mentally, as if their own lives, and not just their future careers, depended on it.

The two sergeants left the office without a word. Green, who had sat quietly through the scene, said: "You were a bit tart there, George."

"I meant to be."

"Why? They've always earned their keep?"

"Because I'm as scared as hell myself, Bill, and we cannot approach this job thinking we're bound to fail before we begin. I'm scared and you've expressed doubts. That attitude must not percolate down to Reed and Berger, nor must it become entrenched in the team."

"I see your point," said Green, "but you've as good as told them it's a nearly impossible job we've taken on."

"If I've done that—without spurring them on to greater efforts than ever before—then I've made a mistake. But to show them we mean business, let's get moving."

"Doing what?"

"The forensic laboratory. Moller said his messengers were collecting the tins last night. I want to see them."

Green got to his feet.

"Seeking inspiration from a bully can?"

"Something of the sort. But before you got down for breakfast this morning, I spent a couple of minutes nosing about in Wanda's pantry."

"And?"

"She had a tin of ham there—an oval shaped one, and a tin of bully and a tin of luncheon meat."

"Ah! Go on."

"Let's see the cans in the laboratory before I say anything else."

"For God's sake," warned Moller, "don't touch them. They're widely separated, as you can see, to prevent cross-contamination. The perspex cheese-dish covers are just added protection."

"You've taken samples from all three."

Moller nodded. "I've got three different bods testing the food scrapings. As we think we know what we're looking for, we can go straight to the positive tests, and so confirmation shouldn't take too long."

"Positive tests, sir?" asked Berger.

"Those that say it is a certain substance, rather than those that say it isn't something else."

"The tins themselves," growled Green. "Have you inspected them?"

"Superficially only so far—for any obvious holes or damage. Really detailed inspection must wait until we're satisfied about the contents. After that we can cleanse them for safe handling."

"That means, in my language, that there's nothing to be seen at first glance."

"Absolutely nothing."

"It's got you worried, doc," accused Green.

"Frankly, yes. Though I said the initial examination was only superficial, it was done extremely thoroughly—in so far as it was possible."

"And there was no hint of a pin-hole."

"None. On any can."

Green turned to Masters. "You had some thoughts about the tins when you looked in your pantry."

"Oh, yes?" enquired Moller. "What were they, Mr Masters?"

Masters leaned against the bench on which he had placed the wide-based brief case he had been carrying and paused for a moment before replying. The others watched him curiously.

"Judging by my wife's store of tinned foods," he began, "at least seventy per cent of all canned foods need a tin-opener to get at the contents."

"A low estimate I'd have said," agreed Moller.

"Another ten per cent are of the type that I will call tear-away tops—Wanda had sardines and a couple of tins of pâté in containers of this sort."

"With you," grunted Green.

"The remaining twenty per cent of all tins are opened with keys

39

supplied by the manufacturer, and all tear out a quarter inch band of metal which is pre-scored in order both to make it an easier operation and to keep the amount of metal that is to be torn away within bounds." He turned to face the bench. "All three of these specimens come within this last category."

"So what, Chief?" asked Berger. "The type is common enough."

"Three out of three from only twenty per cent of the tins on offer?"

"You're right, Masters," said Moller. "By heaven, you're right. You've got to be."

"What the hell are we talking about?" demanded Green.

Masters turned to the bench, opened his briefcase and took out a twelve-ounce tin of corned beef. "Have you a scalpel I could borrow, doctor?"

"Sure." Moller went across to a side bench and returned with the little metal-handled instrument. "That's a new blade, so have a care."

"Thank you." Masters turned the tin on the bench to find the join in the wrap-round label. Carefully, his long slim fingers in complete control of the razor-sharp implement, he eased the seam apart. Then equally carefully, he lifted the paper from the two blobs of brittle, yellow glue and then laid the label asde. "We shall want that later," he murmured.

As he put the scalpel out of harm's way at the back of the bench he said: "Now, gentlemen, the three contaminated tins all have this flap to take the key. But I'm not going to remove my key which, as you can see, is still soldered to the top of the can. It is important that my tin should appear not to have been tampered with, so . . . out of sight, out of mind . . ." With his thumb nail he eased the key flap upwards. "I'm taking care not to bend this so as to make a crease. There's enough natural tension in it just to curve it upwards . . . there, see? Beneath this flap is a less-well finished area. A bit of solder not smoothed out. But the score marks continue up to the seam in the tin."

"Take the solder off," said Moller, "and you expose the score marks which are, by their very nature, a weak part in the plate."

"Right," said Masters. "Weak enough to take the needle of a syringe."

"Not quite," said Green, joining in. "If I was going to do it, I'd make a mark with a pinpoint. An indentation which went half way through . . ."

"Good thinking," said Moller. "Then you'd be less likely to break the point off a fine needle."

Masters continued. "But . . . and it's a big but . . . as soon as the tin is punctured, air will rush in. And we mustn't have any air."

Berger said: "Not necessarily, Chief."

"No?" asked Moller.

"No, doctor. I mean . . . well, what about self-sealing petrol tanks, like on fighter aircraft?"

"Go on," said Masters, "don't stop now."

"Well, Chief, that's done by lining the tanks with rubber. A bullet can go into the tank but the petrol doesn't leak out because the rubber springs back over the hole."

Green nodded. "They brought them in during the Battle of Britain."

Berger continued: "These days, Chief, you can buy tubes of rubber compound from any do-it-yourself shop."

"Rubber solution?"

"Not the old fashioned stuff. It's a bulkier product altogether—for putting round the backs of washbasins and the bases of lavatory pans and so on. It dries very quickly, but remains pliable the whole time." Berger turned to Reed. "You know the stuff. When it first came out they used to stick a blob of it on the card that went with the tube so that you could see what you were buying." He turned back to Masters. "It's watertight and airtight, Chief. If you were to inject through a blob of that before it was dry . . . well, no air would get in and it would seal the hole when you pulled out the needle. When it *was* dry, all you'd have to do would be to rub the blob off, being careful to leave the little plug in the hole."

"Thank you," said Masters.

"Well done, lad," said Green approvingly.

"I can see no reason why it shouldn't work," said Moller, and then added, "sometimes." He looked at Masters. "I think there would only be a small success rate, but that in no way detracts from Sergeant Berger's idea."

"It strengthens it in some ways," said Masters.

"Oh, how, Chief?" asked Reed.

"Use your loaf," counselled Green. "The madman responsible for this caper set out to do the job properly."

"How d'you mean?"

"He wouldn't think three contaminated cans were enough. He'd buy a hundred and try them all. So far, thank God, he's failed on all but three . . ."

"How . . . how do you know he bought a hundred?"

"Feel for the bedpost, lad. I don't know. It could have been a thousand, for anything I know. All I'm saying is he'd have bought a damn sight more than three cans."

"The DCI is right," said Masters. "Our man must have had failures. And Dr Moller thinks— as I do myself—that he would have more failures than successes. And that's a relief, otherwise we might now be faced with dozens of outbreaks of botulism."

"We still could be. Chief. There's no way of telling that all his successes have been placed, or bought, or if bought, used."

"That's right, lad," said Green, "cheer us up."

"But I could be right, couldn't I?"

"You could. You probably are," said Masters. He turned to Moller. "Can I ask you not only to examine these cans for pin holes under the key flaps, but to test a few similar tins yourself in the way Berger described?"

"You bet your life I will. I feel a bit of a clot for not recognising straight off that all these cans are operated by the same mechanism. And if there are holes where you suggest . . ." he gestured towards the three tins under their plastic covers, '. . . just look at where they'll be. Somewhere along those spirals of twisted metal, all jagged edges and, by their very nature, ideally suited to disguise any minute hole along the tear lines."

"If he used rubber to self-seal them, won't that show up in your tests?"

Moller grimaced. "I'd like to give you an emphatic yes to that question, because we reckon we can detect the faintest trace of any substance. And so we can, as long as we can get at it *in situ*. But as I told you, we've got to cleanse those tins before we can inspect them as carefully as we would need to to find a minute plug of rubber."

"You mean the rubber could be washed away?"

"Or melted or jogged out as we straighten those coils of tin. Dammit, it could have been dislodged in the act of opening the tin in the first place. Tearing that metal tape away isn't exactly a gentle business, you know. That's point one."

"There are others?"

"Yes. I don't want to detract from Sergeant Berger's bright idea, but you have to remember that injection needles are hollow. Pushing them through blobs of rubber could bung them up."

"In that case the injection would fail?"

"Not necessarily. But it could mean that more force would have to be put behind the plunger to clear the blockage and force the contaminated broth into the tin."

"Because he had to exert more pressure he would lose some of his control and thus spoil the shot?"

"Either that or he could over-inject. I'm certain he would over-fill his syringe with broth just to cut out the chance of injecting air. So, if the plug were to give way suddenly, before he could stop himself he may have injected more than enough. In that case, the contents of the tin could exert pressure from inside and, when the needle was withdrawn, could start to ooze out through the hole. This would preclude the rubber preparation from forming a bung. Instead, the juices themselves would coagulate and seal the hole. If this happened, there would be no rubber for us to find."

"I see. But the contamination would have been a success?"

"Of course. And if the chap responsible was clever enough to add gelatine to the broth and followed the drill I have just described, that would be likely to be even more successful."

"Still using the blob of rubber?"

"Certainly. He'd have to prevent the initial inrush of air."

"It's all bloody complicated," said Green.

"To a layman, perhaps. But not to someone like me or anybody

43

who worked in a laboratory. We're used to doing fine, fiddly jobs like that.''

Green glanced across at Masters. "He's made your point for you, George.''

"What point is that?" asked Moller.

"When we left the Yard last night, His Nibs said we would be looking for a chemist clever enough to culture botulism who would, at the same time, be a good enough laboratory technician to get it into the tins.''

"On the face of it, that would seem a reasonable supposition.''

"What would?" asked a new voice from the door. As one, they all swung round to face the newcomer. It was Convamore. The pathologist came over to join them. He pushed one of the contaminated tins aside, unceremoniously for such an object, and hefted himself up to sit on the bench.

"Getting anywhere?" he asked Masters.

"That remains to be seen. We've discussed with Dr Moller the method by which we think the contamination could have been introduced into the tins in an inconspicuous manner.''

"Oh? What method is that?"

Convamore listened to the explanation and appeared impressed by it. He went further and said that he himself could certainly suggest nothing more likely though, for form's sake, he thought they must investigate the way the Redcoke depots handled goods to see whether one of them was, in some obscure way, contaminated and, at the same time, capable of transferring such contamination from one set of canned goods to another. "It is highly improbable," he confessed, "but just for laughs we must ascertain whether all these tins did, in fact, pass through the same depot at the same time.''

Green grunted his approval of the logic behind this, but said he doubted the usefulness of such a line of enquiry.

"How do you see it then?" asked Convamore.

"Jiggery-pokery," said Green. "We've got a nutter here, but he's a clever bastard, nonetheless. Not only as far as his knowledge of bugs and his technical laboratory ability are concerned, either. He's a conjurer, too. I reckon he buys his tins and doctors 'em.

44

Buys them quite openly, that is, passing through the check points like any other customer. Then he goes on another shopping spree . . ."

"Not necessarily to the same supermarket," said Reed.

"Right, lad. But when he goes into a Redcoke store, he has a doctored tin with him. Easy enough to do—in a shopping bag. Then he swaps his tin for another of the same sort, or just leaves it. People ditter about like that in supermarkets all the time. They choose goods, then change their minds and put them back and pick up something else. And he can't be nabbed by store detectives—not unless he goes outside with something he hasn't paid for."

"As simple as that, you think?"

"The simpler the better."

"But he gets about—Somerset, Essex, Derby."

"Right, Professor. That makes it difficult for us. He could buy the goods here in London, for all we know. But he doesn't dump them back in the same shop. He travels."

"And that," said Masters, "is a headache for us. There's no anchor point round which we can centre our investigation. We would be looking for a man from any town or village in the country. Had he concentrated his efforts all in one area, we could comb that district for leads. But we haven't got that advantage."

Convamore shrugged. "My job's easier, thank heaven." He turned to Moller. "My body specimens haven't arrived yet, so I'm held up for an hour or two. I shall then be starting saprophytic cultures. I suppose yours are already under way."

"Saprophytic?" queried Masters.

"Sorry. A saprophyte is an organism—like the clostridium bacillus—which lives on dead organic matter."

"Dead?"

"Yes, dead, in so far as all the meat you live on is dead—with the possible exception of oysters, if you ever take them."

"You are culturing the botulism bacteria?" asked Reed.

"We have to, Sergeant, to see if that's what we've got."

"I understand that, sir. But our man—will he know how to do that?"

"Don't ask me."

"Then could I ask you, sir," said Reed, reddening at his own temerity, but determined to show Masters that he was taking an active and intelligent interest in the minutiae of the case, "could I ask you how you culture the . . . saprophytes? So that we know what the bloke we're looking for would have to know?"

"The pleasure's ours," said Convamore. "Mine and Moller's. If you reckon it will help you, we're not going to hold back—certainly not when we get a chance to gas about our own specialities."

"Keep it simple, please," urged Masters.

"The basis of most artificial culture media is nutrient broth," said Convamore. "Broth is broth. Ours is a solution of meat extract. We pep it up a bit to make it better and quicker for our purposes by adding a derived protein and making the whole thing neutral—that is neither salty nor acid. We then add agar, which is an abstraction from Japanese seaweed. It is, chemically, a polysaccharide, and if you want to know what they are, well . . . cellulose and starch are good everyday examples. This helps the broth to solidify more easily on a petri dish or a glass slide. But even better is blood agar. Sounds ghastly, but you know how good the gravy is when you cut a decent joint of beef roasted rare. We use a little horse blood."

"And the bugs thrive on this?"

"Or something like it. I'm going to put cooked and minced beef heart into my nutrient broth. It just happens that organisms of the genus *Clostridia* like it!" He turned to Moller. "Are you using Robertson's meat medium, too?"

Moller nodded. "In a McIntosh and Fiddes jar and in one of the new jars for comparison."

Convamore turned to Masters. "The jar you've just heard about is, these days, an aluminium cylinder which holds several petri dishes with blood agar plates and so on. It's specially made for the culturing of anaerobic organisms. It has an airtight lid with two stop cocks. To one we attach a pump and suck out the air, and to the other we attach a cylinder of hydrogen. The gas enters the jar under pressure and replaces the air. But just to make sure conditions are anaerobic, on the underside of the lid of the jar is a little

46

electric coil which heats some palladium asbestos . . ."

"Palladium being the hard white metal?"

"That's right. It belongs to the platinum group. The palladium asbestos—when heated—acts as a catalyst to cause any little bit of oxygen remaining in the jar to react with the hydrogen to form water. Hey presto! Anaerobic conditions for the little beauties to multiply in."

"And Dr Moller's new jar? What's that like?"

"Much simpler," said Moller. "It has a catalyst that works at room temperature and uses disposable packs of hydrogen. There's no need for gas cylinders and vacuum pumps."

"That's good," said Reed.

"What is?" asked Moller, in some amazement.

"Well, sir, the chap we're looking for will have to do all this culture business himself, won't he? If it's a tricky job with a Mac Something or other's jar . . ."

"No, no," said Masters. "I think you've misunderstood. Professor Convamore and Dr Moller are testing the body organs and the meat cans to see if botulism is actually there. To prove it they have to culture any botulism bacteria which are already in the body fluids—vomit mainly—and the inside scrapings of the tins, to see, first, if botulism is present in both and then to see if the types are the same. That establishes that botulism is the disease, and that it definitely came from these cans. But the man who injected the cans wouldn't have the tricky business of culturing anything in the ways we've just heard."

"No, Chief?"

"Think, Sergeant! Where would he get the material to culture? No, he has to produce his own botulism and from what I can gather, that's the easiest thing in the world, and some people do it by mistake."

"You must be joking, Chief."

"Not at all," said Convamore. "Clostridia are everywhere. When you can meat or vegetables, you have to heat the doings for a long time at a high temperature to kill the spores. But if you can or bottle something and don't heat it for very long and keep the temperature fairly low, you know as well as I do you're asking for trouble. I reckon if you were to put a bit of soil into your cooking, you'd be certain to produce botulism in the stew. And there it is, all ready to be syphoned off and injected into tins of bully, ham and luncheon meat."

Reed scratched his head. Green, seeing his predicament, came to his rescue. "Never mind, lad! Have a fag."

"In here?"

"Why not? I'm sure the boffins won't mind us having a drag while we get a bit more out of them. I'm all at sea myself, you see. So, no doubt, they'll put us right."

"I'd prefer you to come into the office if you want to smoke," said Moller. "Particularly if the Professor is going to light up one of his cigars. All our readings would be shot to hell with everybody puffing away in here."

Convamore dropped from the bench to his feet. "And a cup of coffee, perhaps, young Moller? Or because you're government-employed do you get nothing but tea?"

Moller grinned. "I've educated them round here. We've built our own coffee maker. It's surprising how efficient a brew-machine one can make with a couple of flasks, a funnel, glass tubing, filter papers and a bunsen burner." He turned to Green. "We use beakers, too—the laboratory sort—to drink out of, if there are more people than we have cups for. They're quite good if you hold them in your handkerchief."

"Doesn't worry me, doc. In the desert I had to wire an old tin lid over my mug to keep the flies out of the char. If you've coped with that for a couple of years you can cope with anything."

"I did that," said Convamore. "But I cut my nose on the tin lid and got a desert sore—right on the end of my hooter. Can openers weren't as efficient in those days. They tended to leave jagged edges."

As they moved to Moller's office—one of a number which led off the laboratory—Masters said quietly to the forensic scientist: "They're off. Get together two old boys who served in the desert and you might as well write off the rest of the morning."

"Don't worry. We'll dish up the coffee and then I'll interrupt the reminiscences. We none of us have enough time to fight an old war over again. We've got enough on our hands with the present battle against botulism."

"Thanks."

"Convamore won't mind. He'll be as happy giving you a lecture on pathogenic bacteria as he will discussing the battle of Alamein." He ushered Masters through the office door. "Everybody take a pew where they can. Perhaps one of the sergeants would bring in a couple of bench stools."

Less than five minutes later, Moller had managed to steer the Professor back to the reason for the meeting.

Convamore puffed happily at his cigar and began. "Pathogenic bacteria are those that enter the body tissues to live as parasites and cause disease. Most of them invade the tissues—that is they actually burrow into the flesh or muscle or gut or whatever—and cause inflammation. These little blighters contain certain substances known as endotoxins which help them to invade the body tissues. But there are a few bacteria—some of which invade tissues and some of which don't—which have within themselves extremely powerful poisons known as exotoxins."

"Like poisonous snakes?" asked Masters.

"Exactly. The bacteria with endotoxins can be likened to snakes which will give you a nasty bite but which won't kill you; while those with exotoxins are the ones with a poison that could kill you off pretty quickly if you weren't given an immediate antidote. Good simile, Mr Masters."

Masters inclined his head to acknowledge the compliment. The Professor waved his cigar in the air before beginning again.

"Fortunately, the list of diseases caused by these exotoxins is small. Diphtheria is one—that used to be a killer—scarlet fever another, tetanus another and gas gangrene—the one which caused so many fatalities among wounded men in trench warfare yet another. And that . . ." he took another long draw on his cigar, ". . . brings us to the subject of our present investigation, *Clostridium botulinum*, which little bastard can be absorbed into the tissues through intact intestinal wall to produce botulism." He turned to Green. "Are you with me so far, DCI?"

"I'm getting there," grunted Green.

"What isn't clear?"

"It's clear enough."

"You're sure?"

"Would you like me to recite it back to you?"

Masters interrupted. "We've understood it, Professor. Whether we'll remember it all is a different matter."

"Quite. But as long as you get the salient points and the general drift . . ."

"We'll manage that."

"Excellent. Now, the bacteria themselves. Seen under a very high powered electron microscope, they appear as little rod-shaped bodies with flagella which, as you no doubt know from your police encounters with flagellation, are little whip-like hairs which provide their means of locomotion. The only other thing you need know about them is their peculiar reproductive habits.

"They are primitive micro-organisms and reproduce by binary fission. That means they grow bigger and then split into two. Under favourable conditions, division may be repeated every half hour, so that in less than a day a single organism may become a thousand million. That is not what I meant by peculiar. The next bit is. Under unfavourable conditions a certain number of bacteria form endospores. That's more like a hen developing an egg within itself, because the bacterium does not divide but forms the spore inside its own cell. The spore—like an egg—develops a thick covering layer called a cortex . . ."

"Like the brain of a human?" asked Masters. "A cerebral cortex?"

"Bang on," said the Professor. "A cortex and then a thin but very tough spore coat. As a result, the spores are very resistant to heat. So, though the original bacterium may be killed off by heating to sixty degrees centigrade, the spore will live on, despite its parent's death, until it has been subjected to moist heat at about a hundred and twenty centigrade for ten minutes or more. If it isn't killed off by heating, and the spore finds itself in a favourable environment, it will germinate to form daughter bacteria which soon begin, once more, to divide in the normal way by binary fission. And that, gentlemen, is the story of its life cycle."

"Let me get this straight," said Green. "When it is in soil, that is the unfavourable environment in which it forms spores. When it gets among the meat and veg, that is the favourable environment which makes it reproduce like the clappers."

"I couldn't have put it better myself."

"And these poisons—exotoxins—actually cause a form of intoxication."

"Right. Bacterial intoxication. Where the more popular form of booze-up will cause all the nasties everybody knows about—sickness, loss of co-ordination, double-vision, headache and a hangover—bacterial intoxication from botulism causes vomiting, ocular palsy and throat paralysis. It attacks the nervous system in other words, and all we can do is to inject an anti-serum and provide life support measures for the victims. We hope that these measures will be successful in fifty per cent of patients."

"What serum is it?" asked Masters.

"A polyvalent horse serum. It has to be polyvalent, because we never know which type of botulism is involved. As you were told last night, there are types A to F and each type produces its own exotoxin. Unfortunately, immunity to one will not protect a human from any of the others, and the bloody exotoxin they each produce will pass through a man's intestinal wall like nobody's business. If you want to see how fast the stuff works, visit my lab this afternoon. I shall be injecting mice with blood serum from the affected patients. I've got to do it to make absolutely sure—apart from the symptoms—that the diagnosis of botulism is the correct one. I expect those mice to die of the disease in three or four hours."

"Tough on the mice," grunted Green.

"I don't like doing it, but I've got to. We've not got to make a mistake and let a hitherto unknown disease get among us unsuspected-like."

"Are there any unknown diseases, sir?" asked Berger.

"Well, I'd never heard of Legionnaire's disease until a year or two ago, and as for lassa fever . . ." He spread his hands. "Imported from Africa, but unknown to us."

There were no more questions, so Masters shepherded his team away and back to the Yard.

Chapter 4

"USE MY OFFICE," said Masters to Green, "and have a bit of a brain-storming session for a few minutes."

"What about you?"

"I'm going to see Anderson. I want, if possible, to get him, somehow, to have an official warning issued."

"You heard what he said last night."

"We hadn't discovered then that all the tins were of the strip-open variety. Now, at least, I can ask him to see that people don't use food from tins like that unless they've had them in their homes for some time."

Green looked gloomy. "I'm with you, George, one hundred per cent, but I don't reckon you'll succeed."

"At least I'm going to try. If we can save another family . . ."

"I know all the humanitarian arguments, but the police have no power to forbid people to buy or eat what they want." He looked closely at Masters. "I'm sounding defeatist again, mate, when I should be urging you on. But, honestly, there's something about this business that's griping me. A little kid on holiday eats a bit of ham for tea and next day she's dead and all her family are at death's door. And before we know where we are there'll be other little kids . . . they're already there, in fact, lying helpless with . . . what is it, ocular palsy, paralysis of the throat and puking their little hearts out. This one is different, George. There's been murder done already, but we're out to prevent more murder. It's not a nice little case where we're given a body and somebody says 'There it is. Find out who did it—in your own time.' We haven't got any time at our disposal and yet, because of the nature of the problem, we have to fanny about learning a lot of technical facts just to get ourselves into the picture. It's a galling situation, George."

"Of course it is. Haven't I said I'm worried?"

Green nodded. "I'll join the lads and start talking ideas."

"Try to get some reasonable course of action, Bill, but don't restrain them. Any ideas, however fantastic, should be given an airing. I'll join you shortly."

After Masters had reported on progress, he made his request to Anderson. Could the AC, somehow, arrange for the country to be warned not to use the strip-open cans of food?

Anderson didn't argue. "I'll try," he said. "At six o'clock this evening, there's a TV interview with a doctor from the DHSS. If we could get him to use your discovery to emphasise that the danger lies in that particular type of can—he could use it to show that the authorities really are doing something—every news bulletin would pick it up and it would be noised abroad on radio, and in the newspapers as well as on the screens."

"That should be good enough, sir. Redcoke needn't be mentioned, nor need any specific product."

"Leave it with me. But just one question, George. If we put out a warning against the strip-cans, what's to stop our murderer from contaminating other types of tins?"

"Two things I think, sir. First, the strip-cans have the flap under which to hide a hole and any rubber solution he may use as a bung and second, the score marks for stripping the ribbon of tin are a weakness in the fabric which is ideal for piercing very carefully."

"Moller thinks that a minute hole made under a blob of liquid rubber will not admit air, does he?"

"Not liquid rubber, sir. I don't know the correct term for the state . . . not viscous exactly, not thixotropic either, but soft enough to shape with a knife . . . it will hold its own shape and hold a peak at the top like stiff meringue mixture, and then set like that."

"I see. Well, George, it appears you are getting somewhere. You think you know how the tins are contaminated and you are fairly certain your man is a scientist and a technician with laboratory resources. Right?"

"Throw in some knowledge of the biological sciences as well, sir. A microbiologist or something of that sort."

"Could be a doctor of medicine."

"Perhaps, sir, but few, I would think, are technicians. Dentist perhaps. They have a knowledge of pathology and have to do dexterity work. But we're on the right track, of that I feel sure."

"That's good enough for me. What next?"

"A number of mundane matters, sir."

"Mundane? You've cleared the decks for this one I hope, George?"

"When I said mundane I meant more down-to-earth matters like motives and questioning stores about who buys what. But as for clearing the decks, sir, Green and I were not on call—nowhere near the top of the list—so we were separately engaged on general work. We'll have to tie things up."

"Drop everything. Put all your files in the Commander's office—both of you. I want this botulism business to be given absolute top priority."

"Right, sir."

"Have you set up an Incident Room?"

"No, sir. There is no focal point to the case, as yet. I just can't see checks and cross-checks paying off until we have narrowed down the area of search to more manageable proportions. Until some of the patients are well enough to give us some information as to where they bought their respective tins, we won't even know which stores to look at. For instance, sir, if the people who were camping in Somerset stocked up with food before setting out for their holiday, their tin of ham could have been bought in a town the other end of the country, so I don't want to waste time in Taunton."

"I see your point, George, but keep a careful file. We want to be able to tie up the bits and pieces."

Masters grinned. Anderson continued: "And don't smirk like that, George. Your usual files are more noteworthy for their brevity and slimness than their comprehensiveness. This time everybody will want everything."

Masters got to his feet. "I'll see to it, sir."

When he reached his office, Reed was talking.

"There's got to be a motive. Even nutters have motives that seem reasonable to themselves, if not to anybody else."

"Go on," said Masters, crossing to his chair. "Don't let me stop you."

"Well, Chief, all I'm asking is, what is our chap aiming to do? He can't be going for the people who have now got the disease, because he won't know any of them—or if he does, it's going to be a hell of a coincidence."

"Not necessarily," said Berger. "If he put one of his tins in his local store, it could be that one of his neighbours would buy it a couple of minutes later."

"Hold it," said Green. "We don't know where any of the patients come from. We know the Burnham family were on a camping holiday, so we assume they came from somewhere outside Somerset. But we don't know anything about the people in the Colchester and Derby hospitals. Do they live in those areas? Or are they on holiday, too, away from home? If they are it could be that they all got their provisions at the same shop."

"That would be a turn up for the book."

"Maybe, lad. But it's a possibility."

"It's something we have to resolve," said Masters. "Make a note, Reed. Phone all three hospitals or the local nicks and get the names and addresses of every botulism patient. Then we can think about that particular point with some information to go on."

"Right," said Green. "Sarn't Reed was talking about motive. He doesn't reckon the object of this exercise was to kill off the people . . ."

"It was," said Reed.

"You just said it wasn't, lad."

"Not the primary object perhaps and not necessarily those specific people. But I do reckon our nutter set out to kill a number of people, no matter who they were . . ."

"Why?" asked Berger.

"To get at Redcokes." replied Reed.

"You mean," asked Masters, "that the primary target in this man's mind was Redcoke Stores?"

"Yes, Chief."

"So his motive was what? To square some grievance with the owners of Redcoke?"

"I reckon so, Chief."

"You sound very positive."

"Why would he make a point of buying his tins from Redcoke Stores, if Redcoke wasn't to be his victim?"

"Because it was his local shop," said Berger.

"And then he travelled round the country leaving them in other Redcoke stores? No, mate. A bloke as clever as this wouldn't foul his own nest. He wouldn't go to any of his own local shops where he could be well known, if not to the shopkeepers, at any rate to chance customers. He'd travel, this boyo. And after travelling, he made for the Redcoke store in the town he'd stopped at to buy his tins."

"Why Redcokes? Why not Sainsbury's or Tesco's or the International?" asked Berger.

"That's my point. The others are all there, but he went to Redcokes."

"He just happened to hit on Redcokes. He wanted a big chain that had branches all over the country so he could drop his doctored tins anywhere he felt like it. Any chain would have suited his purpose."

Reed scratched his head, and Green said: "Come on, lad. You started this motive lark. Young Berger is tying you up in knots."

"Look," said Reed desperately. "The nutter was not out to kill specific people. We know that, because the method he chose was definitely non-specific. Right?"

"Right."

"But killing these people had to serve some specific purpose. Right?"

"We'll agree on that for the moment."

"Thanks. Well, what other specific objective is there? If not the people, it must be the Redcoke chain of stores. He's got it in for them for some reason." Reed looked across at Green. "That's my argument."

"Bloody good, too," said Green. "When you arrived at it." He turned to Berger. "Have you got anything to support that instead of shooting it down?"

"Only that I'm more convinced than I was."

"That's summat." Green turned to Masters. "George?"

"For what it's worth at the moment, I'll back Reed. And I'll tell you why. Dr Moller gave it as his opinion that the nutter would try to contaminate a lot of tins—we actually mentioned a hundred, remember—and would fail with most of them. Now I reckon that a chap who is going to buy up a hundred tins to doctor isn't going to get them all from the same place."

"Obvious," growled Green.

"And I can't see why he should get them from the same chain either, unless he had to."

"Go on, Chief," said Reed.

"If he wasn't particular, he would buy his tins from several stores in smaller lots. Those tins he successfully managed to contaminate would then be returned to branches of the store from which they were bought. This would have to happen, not only because the different chains sell different brands in many cases, but because the price labels usually carry the name of the store."

"A price label wouldn't matter, Chief. He could remove them. You often find the odd tin not priced."

Masters shook his head. "Sorry, Berger, but I won't buy that—although what you say is true about missing price tags."

"Why not, Chief?"

"Simply because an unpriced article at check-out becomes the object of scrutiny. We've all experienced it. The girl on the till looks at every face of the tin, searching for the missing label. Our man would, I suggest, prefer not to have his handiwork examined, no matter how carefully he had done his stuff. He would much rather it was nonchalantly pushed along the counter without a second glance."

"True," said Green. "And there's another thing I should tell you in this connection. My missus won't take a tin or packet that isn't priced. I've seen her put an unpriced one back and take another that is priced. And if my missus does that, I'd like to bet there's thousands of other women who do the same thing, so's they're not overcharged at the till."

"Good point," said Masters. "I'm positive our man would want his doctored goods to look as normal as possible—for all the

57

reasons stated. So, to get back to my support for Reed's contention that the prime target is Redcoke. If our chap bought a great many tins from various chains, it would strike me as odd that all his few successes were with tins that came from one chain only." He held up his hand to forestall interruptions. "I would accept that oddity if all his successes were with one particular type of tin from one particular chain. But I cannot accept it when his successes come from different types of tin all from the same chain. Therefore I believe all his tins came from Redcoke stores and since he made a point of getting them all from Redcoke stores, he had a good reason for doing so. And that reason, I submit, like Reed, leads me to believe that Redcoke was intended to be his prime victim."

Green rubbed his pudgy nose with one finger, and said apologetically: "George, I didn't do any of the thought processes, but I arrived at the same answer. I just assumed Chummy was out to clobber Redcoke."

"It as obvious as that?"

"To me, yes."

"I'm not going to knock your flashes of inspirational genius."

"No . . ."

"Something is worrying you."

"I'm not sure either of us is right."

"Neither am I, but we have to start somewhere, and at least we have a basis—arrived at both by inspiration and logic—for action. We'll soon know if we're wrong, and quite honestly, Bill, we've got to do something. Moreover, we would have to test all possibilities, and Redcoke would figure among those anyway. All we've done is to decide to give them high priority."

"With no alternatives," said Berger wryly.

Masters looked across at him. "There are, you know: conjectural ones—even highly speculative. But we can't move until we get facts. You touched on one of them—what if all the patients shopped in the same store? Is our man out to get a number of local people or just to do the dirt on that one store or, say, its manager?" Masters spread his hands. "Go even further. We all refer to Mister Botulism as a nutter. A crank, in other words. He's poisoned meats only, so far. What if he's a raving vegetarian trying to drive people away from ham or beef? Or one of those people who want to stop us slaughtering animals for food? Or . . ."

"Don't go on," begged Green. "The lads get the picture and my belly's beginning to think my throat's cut. I'm that hungry I could eat a dish of sheeps' eyeballs."

"Without batting an eyelid," murmured Berger.

"At least they don't can them," said Green.

Masters got to his feet. "Be back here as soon as you can. There's work to be done."

They re-assembled within three-quarters of an hour. Reed and Berger had eaten fish and chips in their canteen. Masters and Green had chosen bread and cheese and a pint of beer in a nearby pub.

"I had calls put through to the three nicks, Chief. We've got the answers."

"What are they?"

"Mr and Mrs Burnham live in Ewell in Surrey, and they bought their tinned food in Kingston before going on holiday. They have two—had two—kids, as you know.

"Mr and Mrs Oliver live in Colchester and they shopped there. They are the only two affected there.

"Mr and Mrs Seymour live in Derby and shop there. But there are four of them ill. Mr and Mrs Geary had a meal with them. Mrs Geary is their daughter."

"Thank you. That means that our man operates over a wide area and so we can rule out any ideas we may have had that he was hoping to affect any particular group of local people, or to harm one particular Redcoke store or its manager."

Green grunted his agreement. Masters packed his pipe as he continued. "The head office of Redcoke Stores is here in London. I know very little about their operation, but I'm of the impression that they have spread their wings—in common with all other supermarket chains—over the past few years. Nor am I a business man knowing much about property deals. But again I'm of the impression that there's a lot of wheeling and dealing over the acquisition of prime sites for even bigger big shops. It is not beyond the bounds of possibility that some small-property owners have been treated in a manner which they may consider to be less than just during the arranging of some of these deals."

"That's about the strength of it," conceded Green. "There's a lot of duck-shoving in the property market. Tenants booted out of their homes and businesses so that the landlord can get a good price for vacant possession. That sort of thing."

"It seems a fruitful area for investigation. So I want us to seek the help of the Redcoke head office . . ."

"To expose any crooked property deals they've been involved in?" asked Green scornfully. "You'll get as much joy out of that as a Hottentot gets from a witchdoctor's curse."

"You'll manage, Bill."

"Me? I see. The tricky bit is being left to me, is it?"

"You'll manage. All that has to be done is to ask them for the addresses of all their new supermarkets for the last five years. Then . . ."

"Why five years?"

"Do you think this hate would go back longer than that?"

Green grimaced. "It could fester. It's probably been building up in our nutter. Over a long period."

"I'll leave it to your discretion, Bill, but don't forget that these huge stores take anything up to a couple of years to build, so going back five years could be, in effect, going back seven."

Green grunted to show he had appreciated the point.

"And I don't want to make the operation too big."

"What operation?"

"We are going to investigate every one of those sites—who lost his land or business or whatever—to try and unearth somebody with a grievance against Redcoke."

Green helped himself slowly to a Kensitas from a crumpled packet. Then he said: "It's not our scene, George. Country-wide enquiries on a big scale . . . it's a long routine job . . . there are others who are better at it than we are."

"We've been given the job."

"To get a quick result. The sort of investigation you're proposing could take months—a Yorkshire Ripper job." Green got up to put a dead match in the ashtray. "Come on, mate. You're a fast worker. Let's have something else."

Masters replied: "I'm having two strings to this bow. The slow, routine one, and our usual method of working." He grimaced. "Because I can't guarantee success by working as we usually do, and we simply have to succeed."

"Because there may be other lives at stake, Chief?" asked Reed.

"Precisely. Normally it doesn't matter if it takes us two days or two weeks to find a murderer. But this time . . . the bastard may be planting tins at this moment."

"Good enough," said Green rising to his feet. "Get the address of the Redcoke office, laddo," he said to Berger, "and get a car pronto. We're on our way." As Berger left the office, the DCI turned to Masters. "What about you, George?"

"We're going to have to set up an Incident Room," said Masters reluctantly.

"Where?"

"Here. There's nowhere else. I've decided to ask for a uniformed Inspector and a couple of clerks to run it. I don't want all the usual Church Hall paraphernalia, but we will have to be able to co-ordinate those property searches. There'll be the technical material coming in, too."

"You'll have to deal with that yourself."

"I intend to. That's why I hope you'll take charge of the property business. I'll see you when you get back from Redcoke."

Green shrugged and went off.

"What about me, Chief?" asked Reed.

"I want you to go shopping."

"Chief?"

"Get a car and a plain-clothes driver, and get round to every Redcoke store you can manage between now and closing time. Buy one tin of anything at each store."

"Why, Chief?"

"Just do it. And get back here by six or soon after. And get out into the suburbs."

Reed went about his business.

*

61

Masters had spent more than an hour arranging the setting up of the Incident Room. The uniformed staff members who were to help him had been briefed and started on their various tasks. By the time all three were installed, together with a couple of small tables for desks, there was very little room left in Masters' office, but it was as he wanted it. He felt the need to be close—physically as well as mentally—to everything that was going on.

Keith Lake, the Inspector who had been lent to him, was an intelligent young man. He lacked the experience that is so great an asset in setting up the checking and cross-checking procedures that are usually so vital in the sifting out of clues in a case of this nature, but Masters was content to have a man who might well understand more of the technical side of the investigation than one who would be left to juggle his clues in the darkness of incomprehensibility.

"I have a job for you personally, Lake."

"Sir."

"I want a file on botulism. By that, I mean a photocopy of every paper written on it that you can find. The library here, the boffins, the Royal Society of Medicine Library and any other source you can think of. Glance through them as you go so that you don't duplicate the material. By that, I mean, go to one good pathology book and take their section on the basic information, and don't get any others that are similar. Have it here by six o'clock if you can. At least have something here. I want to do some homework tonight."

"Understood, sir."

Masters was in the process of explaining to one of the two remaining policemen how he wanted a map of the country set up, when a call from Anderson came in.

"George, the doctor from the DHSS—the one who is broadcasting at six—is in my office. I think you'd better come up here and meet him."

"Right away, sir."

Masters' first thought when he was introduced to Dr Cutton was that he was the last man he himself would consider putting up as a spokesman for the Ministry. Not that the doctor was ill-favoured, but rather that his manner was of that irritating variety that puts up the backs of colleagues and causes them to dislike those who may be perfectly able, even brilliant men. Masters got that far on introduction. Before the conversation was more than a minute or two old, the Chief Superintendent found his initial repugnance to the man growing stronger.

"The Assistant Commissioner tells me you would like me to warn the public against using tinned meat that comes in the strip-open cans."

"As a measure of safety, Doctor. All three of the contaminated cans are of that variety. I realise we cannot be sure that any further cans—should there be any—will be the same, but at least by issuing such a warning we may save some lives."

Cutton shook his head. "Can't be done, Masters."

"Can't be done?" Masters' tone sounded dangerous. Anderson stepped in quickly. "I have already asked Dr Cutton to take the steps you suggest, George. It is because he has refused to issue a warning that I asked you to meet him—so that you would know at first-hand why your apparently reasonable request has been refused."

Masters was certain that Anderson had as poor an opinion of Cutton as he himself had—and obviously arrived at equally quickly. "Certainly I should like to be told why Dr Cutton takes the attitude he has chosen to adopt. My business, as a policeman, is to save life wherever possible and to try to do so however slim the chance. Equally I would have thought that to have been the objective of the medical profession, too."

"Now, George," warned Anderson. "Hear Cutton out before getting too cross."

"Quite," said Cutton, self-importantly. Masters squirmed inwardly. The man was dressed well, in pale grey, with a reasonable shirt and tie. His hair was cut relatively short and everything else about him measured up except the insufferable manner and, perhaps, a sort of lippy-toothed slew to the mouth as he spoke. "Now," he continued, "we at the Ministry don't want you people to make too much of this botulism scare. I shall tell the public tonight that botulism is so rare that the chances of anybody contracting it are millions to one against."

"Naturally, perhaps," said Masters quietly. "But with a madman loose . . ."

"That's just the point. We can't say there is a madman loose. First because we have no proof that there is, and second because such a statement, even if proven, would cause panic. I therefore take the view that I cannot suggest to the public that there is anything out of the ordinary going on. Were I to do so, the result would be disastrous. So I cannot give a blanket warning against all strip-open cans. Were you able to give me a single batch number for one single food, the situation would be different."

"You could warn them against Redcoke products in strip-open cans," suggested Anderson.

"Impossible. The effect on one of the largest food stores in the country would be disastrous, and the action they could take—and win—were I even to hint that their items, and theirs alone, were responsible for the outbreak, would cause so great a legal furore that we at the Ministry shudder to contemplate it."

"It would most probably save lives," insisted Masters.

"Not so. It would jeopardise far more lives than it would save."

"How on earth do you make that out, Dr Cutton?" demanded Anderson.

Cutton smirked. "A little thought would give you the reason. Or perhaps you are too isolated from the public to gauge their reaction to a warning that particular Redcoke foods may be dangerous?"

"Tell us," grated Anderson, visibly angry.

"Everybody—and there would be millions of them—who had eaten food taken recently from a Redcoke strip-can, would immediately feel ill. Such is the power of suggestion, particularly on television. Within an hour, every doctor in the country would be overwhelmed with patients who thought they felt ill or who wanted a check-up 'just in case'. A GP who failed to recognise a genuine case after the patient had reported to him would be vilified—and worse. So doctors would take samples of blood, and every path lab in the country would be so swamped with unnecessary tests that the ordinary routine hospital tests—most of them vital—would be skimped or overlooked or delayed in the flood of work. The work of hospital doctors would be held up, and the patients would suffer, probably to the point where fatalities ensued. That is what I meant when I said that to utter a warning about Redcoke strip-cans could well cause more deaths than it would prevent."

Masters and Anderson remained silent when Cutton had finished. Their lack of response seemed to urge him to make a further statement. "Surely you can see that even if I mentioned Redcoke products, a great many people would take that to mean any strip-cans. They would either forget the qualification, or they would say that all the shops sell the same goods with different labels and the results I have just described would apply to and spring from the contents of any of that particular type of can. You're warning is not on, Masters."

Masters ignored Cutton and addressed himself direct to Anderson. "Isn't it possible to appeal to a slightly higher authority, sir?" he asked quietly.

It was a calculated insult, and Cutton took it as such. His anger flared. "I didn't come here . . . " he began.

"Steady, gentlemen, steady," ordered the AC sternly. "You both have right on your side. You, George, to want to do everything to save life, and you, Doctor, to want to save the whole medical world from being cast into turmoil. You've both had your say. Now I suggest we forget it. George, I think you'd better get back to your investigation and please don't try to circumvent the DHSS policy by making your own point to the press through Moller. Is that understood?"

"I understand, sir."

"Thank you."

Masters, seething with rage, returned to his office. Shortly afterwards Green joined him.

"I've been to the Redcoke head office, George."

"What did you find out?"

"Wait a moment, mate. What's the matter with you?"

Masters grimaced. "I've just had a most unpleasant interview with a Dr Cutton from the Ministry. The man had the most irritating manner. Smug, I suppose you'd call it."

"I see," said Green. "He got up your nose because he regards himself as the Great I Am whereas you know that you already hold that unique position?"

Masters grinned ruefully. "You could be right. Actually he's the one making the TV appearance tonight and he turned down flat my request for a warning against Redcoke strip-cans."

"Just like that?"

"To be fair to him, he produced some reasoned arguments about panicking the public and swamping the health service, but it was the way he did it and his manner that flicked me on the raw. To be candid, Bill, I wanted to hit him."

Green regarded him closely for a minute.

"Then he must have really upset you, George, because I've never before heard you say that. I reckon it's a measure of how worried you are by this case."

"Worried isn't the word for it. I've been thinking . . ."

"The worst thing you could do."

"Thinking over what was said this morning."

"There was a hell of a lot said."

"About how the botulism that was used in the cans came to be made in the first place."

"You heard what Convamore said."

"And I know what I told Reed. That it would be easy to produce clostridia because people do it inadvertently all the time."

"Right. And Convamore agreed."

"So he did. But I don't think he's ever produced any himself—I can see no reason why he should have done. He's merely cultured it *after* it has contaminated something."

"After it is already alive and kicking, you mean?"

Masters nodded. "And he isn't a detective—or at least not our sort. I don't believe he's considered anything from our point of view so far. Only from his own."

"What the hell are you getting at, George?"

Masters began slowly to fill his pipe. "What I think I am trying to say, Bill, is that to produce botulism bugs is easy enough, but to produce them in isolation could be extremely difficult. That is why I believe what I said to Reed this morning is wrong."

"And what Convamore said?"

"Is wrong, too."

"Go on."

"Convamore is an authority on this, and I'm most definitely not. But I have been brought up to believe that if you don't cook meat well enough to kill off all the bugs, the food remains infected and there is every chance of the danger of bacterial multiplication."

Green stared at him. "That's exactly what everybody has been saying the whole time."

"Yes, they have. But if your missus undercooked a bit of stew and you got tummy-ache because of it, you wouldn't expect the ailment to be botulism, would you?"

"No . . . o," said Green slowly. "I'd expect it to be gut's ache—gastroenteritis—due to food poisoning."

"Caused by what organisms?"

"Salmonella—isn't that the name?"

Masters tapped the table, waiting for Green's thought processes to catch up. At last—"You're on to something, George . . ."

"You see what I'm getting at?"

"Of course I see what you're getting at. If our laddo produced his botulism soup, stew, hash or ragout—as it says on the sauce bottles—he would be producing other food-poisoning organisms at the same time. And all the others, except botulism, produce diarrhoea—according to Convamore and Moller. So . . ." Green paused as if for breath. "So . . . if all the present patients haven't got diarrhoea and gut's-ache, the botulism bug must have been produced in isolation. And as we have no reports that the patients have got the trots . . . we haven't, have we?"

"No. I'm going to get Lake to ring round the hospitals to confirm it, though."

"Per-zactly." Masters grinned at Green's valiant efforts to cheer him up. "So we are back to our first thought. We're looking for an illegitimate glow-worm."

"A what?"

"A bright bastard. A scientist-cum-technician as opposed to any old bod. Somebody who can produce the botulism organism without the other nasties." Green took out a battered Kensitas. "So what are you getting worried about, mate? You've just uncovered something mighty important. That shows you are on top, or at least coping with the job. What more do you want? The ability to solve the riddle inside five-and-twenty minutes?"

Masters smiled. "I wouldn't mind."

"I'll bet you wouldn't."

Masters called across to one of the uniformed constables. "Could we have some tea, please," and then turned back to Green. "Sorry, Bill. I haven't even had the courtesy to ask how you got on at Redcoke HQ."

"Doesn't matter."

"What doesn't?"

"Your not asking. You knew the answer before I went. I've always said you were jammy. I'll wager everything I've got that you know nothing about the running of supermarkets or grocery chains."

"I don't."

"But yet you could tell me Redcoke would have built, on average, five big stores a year for the past five years."

"It was a guess, Bill. I didn't tell you they had."

"Good. Because if you had, you'd have been wrong—by two. They've actually knocked up twenty-three."

"Widespread around the country?"

"John o' Groats to Land's End."

"That makes our job more difficult, I suppose."

"Not it. I'm not visiting them."

"Telex messages to the local nicks?"

Green shook his head. "A personal phone call. I can say what I mean in a person-to-person chat."

The constable put two cups of tea on the desk. Green tasted his and grimaced. "You trying to poison me, lad? There's no sugar in this."

"Sorry, sir. Didn't know you took it."

"Thought I was sweet enough without, did you? Well, you were wrong, so let's have a couple of spoonsful from somewhere, lad."

As the constable left, Masters asked: "If I were you, I'd jot down a check list of what you're going to ask over the phone. After all, you'll have to do it twenty-three times, so it would be better to get the same message across each time. Then Lake can keep the list to make sure he gets all the answers when they're phoned in."

"Right. But there'll be no common form of questions and answers. I want the locals to find out whether old, empty property was demolished, whether currently used property was absorbed, open ground—all that sort of thing. Then I want to know about prices paid. Was some little owner gypped? Or frightened out?"

"Or had his view spoilt? Or his peace and quiet ruined by the hordes of shoppers that suddenly arrived outside his windows? It hasn't got to be purely a monetary blow that somebody suffered."

"That's right. They opened up an all-night launderette near us—on the corner where the paper shop was. Now not only can we no longer get papers, fags, cards and all the rest, but we have cars stopping and starting all night and women tapping about in those wooden-heeled shoes. Besides, the activity there has started to draw the yobs. They congregate there. Some went in and beat the place up a week or two ago. I know I'd like to do somebody for turning a decent, traditional amenity into nothing more than a damned nuisance."

"Have you done anything about it?"

Green shrugged. "I asked the locals to keep an eye open. But the only thing that would work would be to revoke the all-night licence."

Masters grinned. "I've a better idea, Bill."

"What's that?"

"Why don't you buy the premises and turn them back into a newsagent's shop?"

Green frowned and then suddenly straightened in his chair. "Do you know, George, that's not a bad idea."

"Are you serious?"

"Why not? I haven't got all that long to go, and Doris has always wanted a little shop. She used to work in one, you know, before we were married."

"And her lifelong ambition has been to own a shop of her own?"

Green nodded. "I've never done anything about it, but there's no reason . . . I shall have to do something, won't I? I'll mention it to her. At least it will give her something to think about."

"Newsagents have to get up early—every day."

"And I suppose a copper doesn't have unsocial hours?"

"That's true."

"There's a house behind and above the shop. If we sold ours . . ."

"Steady," warned Masters. "Don't go too fast, and don't you dare tell Doris that I suggested it. I was joking."

"I know."

"Good. Now to get back to this case . . ." He was interrupted by the constable putting a bowl of sugar on the desk.

"You've been so long, lad, it's cold by now," said Green, helping himself to a heaped spoonful."

"Sorry, sir."

Masters began again. "Bill, besides the property deals, there's another aspect I want you to look at. We must explore the disgruntled employee angle. There could be some chap whom Redcoke has got rid of and who thinks he was treated less than fairly. Get the locals to inquire into that, too."

"I'll ask them," replied Green, "but I don't think they'll get very far with that one. They won't know anything about any of the internal politics of Redcoke."

"Maybe not, but they could make discreet inquiries among other members of staff. And they would know if Redcoke had ever prosecuted an employee for theft."

"We're getting deeper, George."

"I suppose the list of possibilities is endless, Bill, but we've got to do it. How else are we to proceed if we don't assume for the moment that this is a hate campaign directed at Redcoke?"

"We've got to assume that. But I can't see a chap who is an able scientist and technician being an ex-employee of a grocery chain which has treated him badly. But I do reckon he could have been a property owner who was diddled."

"We daren't overlook anything, Bill."

Green got to his feet. "Berger is reserving two open lines in my office. I'll get on with the phoning, and I'll write a confirmatory memo to each of the forces I speak to. They'll go off tonight."

"Thanks."

*

70

"I've brought in a portable TV, sir," said Lake. "So that you can see the broadcast at six."

"Thank you. Let Mr Green and Sergeant Berger know. I'd like them to see it."

"Right, sir."

"By the way, how many enquiries have we had from the press?"

"Only three direct to us here, sir. Most are going through the press office. I'm just telling callers to contact Dr Moller, as you instructed."

"Quite right. I was really wanting to know the amount of interest the outbreaks have caused. Various people have suggested there could be panic and I was wondering just how true that could be."

"I could open a file specifically for reaction reports, sir. I'll have the PR clippings boys send us newspaper reports and we can tape radio and TV. We could build up a full dossier—including letters to the papers. There'll be some of those tomorrow, for sure."

"In that case . . ."

The phone rang on Masters' desk. Lake picked it up and answered. After listening for a moment, he handed it over to Masters. "Dr Moller, sir." As Masters took the handset, Lake called over to one of his subordinates. "Log a call for now from Dr Moller to DCS Masters. Get Mr Masters' note of the contents after he's finished speaking."

The centre was working. Resignedly Masters took up pencil and pad. He supposed he'd better jot down whatever Moller had to say.

"Masters."

"Hello, there. Harry Moller here. I've rung to tell you that I and two lab technicians have been trying out the method of infecting cans that was suggested by your Sergeant."

"Any luck?"

"Some. We tried a case of four dozen cans, and reckon we got five, possibly six, successes."

"That at least suggests that the method is feasible."

"It is, without a doubt, and I feel it safe to say that we would achieve a slightly higher percentage of successes the longer we continued."

"You mean you would become more adept?"

"Quite. We were learning just how the materials had to be handled. But I thought you would like to know that we have had a better than ten per cent success so far."

"So far? You propose to go on?"

"My people here have been injecting uncontaminated broth, of course."

"Testing the mechanics only?"

"Quite. Now we are facing the next problem, and that is going through the same motions with anaerobes."

"You mean what you've done so far is no good?"

"Not good enough, in my opinion."

"Why not?"

"Because we think that we're not getting a completely airtight job. We think that if we were to use a hydrogen bottle to activate the syringe, for example, at least those successes we got would be anaerobic."

"I see. Thanks for letting me know. And by the way, what sort of questions have you been asked by reporters?"

"I held one short session for them this afternoon. I'm sorry to tell you, old chap, that they are a darned sight more interested in the clinical side of the attack than they are in the police and forensic efforts to stop it recurring."

"Thank heaven for that. It means there is no panic."

"None at all, so far. I don't think they've got round to the causes and implications."

"Good. Did you know that a Dr Cutton of the DHSS is broadcasting on television at six this evening?"

"Nobody ever tells me anything."

"We have a set in my office if you care to come along."

"I might just do that. If so I'll be there in about twenty minutes."

"We'll be pleased to see you."

After ringing off, Masters completed his telecon for the file and handed it across to one of Lake's assistants. He had scarcely put down his pencil before the phone rang again.

Convamore.

"Good afternoon, Professor."

"Masters, my boy, bad news."

"What sort of bad news? Another outbreak?"

"How did you guess?"

"For there not to be more seemed too good to be true. Where this time?"

"Bournemouth. A crowd in a self-catering flatlet. Four adults and three children. There was a baby there, too, but it wasn't fed the meat loaf."

"That again? I take it you are referring to the Redcoke luncheon meat?"

"The same. Fortunately, they were able to get help pretty quickly by knocking up people in the neighbouring flat, and the health authorities there, alerted by knowledge of the previous outbreaks, immediately suspected botulism and took the necessary steps."

"What are they?"

"Massive doses of botulinum antitoxin. As the type of botulism was unknown to the hospital doctor, he played safe and gave them a tri-valent anti-serum against types A, B and E. With the usual life support measures to help them breathe and so on, that particular group should pull through because they're all young and healthy."

"Did you tell us earlier that the antitoxin was a polyvalent horse serum?"

"That's right."

"What is the availability of the antitoxin?"

"Meaning?"

"Is enough of it readily available all over the country? With outbreaks of botulism occurring almost everywhere, heaven knows where and when it will be needed."

"Don't worry about that side. Every area is catered for."

"Amply catered for?"

"Every major hospital carries stocks and the manufacturers have assured us they have stocks at their distribution points. They can be rushed anywhere."

"I'm pleased to hear it, because when you started talking about

73

the Bournemouth people giving massive doses to seven patients . . . what I mean is, surely they don't carry that much stock of a drug which is needed so rarely and, presumably, has a shelf-life of only a few years?"

"I've checked up on it," replied Convamore. "Personally, I mean. I think you—and everybody—can rest assured that we have adequate stocks of the anti-serum, and to make doubly sure, the manufacturers started up a production line this afternoon. If, by any chance after that, we find ourselves running short, we shall fly in ear-marked stocks from the States. Three hours away by Concorde, chum."

"So somebody has pulled his finger out in that direction, at least."

"What's up, young Masters? Why so bitter?"

"I've had a meeting with a chap from the DHSS, a Dr Cutton . . ."

"Ah! The prize Mugwump himself! Detestable in his mugwumpery, ain't he?"

"You describe him so well. I can only assume you have encountered him."

"Encountered is the right word. But you will probably find that it was he who took the steps you were just applauding—seeing that we have adequate stocks of the horse serum."

"That doesn't alter my opinion of him. We have yet to see what he says in his broadcast. He refused our request to issue any form of warning."

"Did he, indeed? Ah, well, it's what I'd expect of him. But to return to our little botulism, I thought you'd like to know that all the samples I've tested are exclusively type E—if it's any help to you."

"Thank you. The knowledge may be useful."

Green and Berger came in as Masters finished his notes on this conversation. "Ready for the show, George? There's only a couple of minutes to go."

"Ask Lake to switch on."

Masters told Green of the fourth outbreak while the set was warming up, and just as Cutton was announced, Moller joined them.

"Made it," he gasped. "Nearly didn't. News of the fourth case came in."

Masters nodded and they settled down to listen to Cutton.

He spoke for about four minutes. Nobody uttered a word until he had finished.

"Patronising bastard," said Moller.

"Have you met him?"

"No, and I can't say I wish to."

"He didn't say a bloody thing," grunted Green. "Don't worry, all will be well. No danger. We're looking after it. Botulism is so rare that the chances of getting it are millions to one against! We don't need many more incidents the size of the Bournemouth one before the chances will fall to less than *one* million to one." He turned to Masters. "We're supposed to have progressed a long way in the last forty years, but we're now considered to be too immature to be told of blood, sweat and tears, even if the trouble is likely to last for only five days instead of five years."

Masters nodded. "I can't agree with feeding facile pap of that sort to the public, with no hint as to how to protect themselves." He picked up the outside phone. "I'm going to ring Redcoke head office," he declared grimly, "and say to them that as four of their damned strip-cans have so far caused—how many? . . . about twenty?—cases of botulism in the past twenty-four hours, it is time they withdrew the remaining stocks from their shelves."

"That won't help people who have already bought infected tins," reminded Moller.

"No it won't," grunted Green as Masters asked the switchboard to get his number, "but at least it will stop more being sold."

Masters was hanging on to the phone. After some delay, the operator informed him there was no reply from Redcoke.

"It's way after six o'clock, Chief," said Berger. "Those offices will have been empty since half past five."

Masters put the phone down in disgust.

"Just as well," said Moller. "By tomorrow we could be in a position to force their hand. If we want to, that is," he said looking round.

"How?"

"Well, when I hold a press conference tomorrow, I could have the cans on display for the photographers to snap and the correspondents to draw their own conclusions from. I won't have to mention the name, Redcoke . . ."

"I like it, Doc," said Green. "Have a tube." He offered the scientist his packet of Kensitas.

"Then nobody gets in the soup," continued Moller, accepting the cigarette. "All I have to say is that those are the cans from which my team and I have collected the botulism bacteria. That is the truth and nobody can blink that."

"It's come to something," complained Masters, "when people like us have to stoop to that sort of caper in order to get one of the country's leading enterprises to do the humane thing." He turned to Moller. "I'd like to give them the chance to do it off their own bat before we force their hand."

"Okay. You've got until eleven tomorrow morning. That's the time of the press conference."

"Hold it, hold it," protested Green. "Do it off their own bat, George? How would we know? They wouldn't publicise it. Or were you thinking of nudging them tomorrow morning and getting a promise from them?"

"That was my intention."

"And it's a good one. But if you have to prompt them you can hardly call it doing it off their own bat."

"No matter, if it succeeds."

"Fair enough," said Moller getting to his feet. "Let me know how you get on—before eleven o'clock. Oh, and incidentally, George, all the cans have yielded E type."

"Exclusively?"

Moller nodded.

"No salmonella?"

"No. Why should there be?"

"Think it over, Doctor. Goodnight."

As Moller left, Reed entered the room. "Sorry I'm late, Chief, but I thought I'd better finish the job." He put two plastic carriers bulging with tins of food on the desk. "There's something of interest here, I reckon."

"What?" demanded Green.

"Price tickets," murmured Masters quietly.

"You knew, Chief?" exclaimed Reed.

"That they differed between tins? Yes. What I didn't know was whether they differed between stores." He turned to Green. "The tin I took from Wanda's shelf this morning had a label which was rectangular with an indented semicircle at each end. At least one of the tins on Moller's bench had a rectangular label with rounded corners. I couldn't see the others, and I couldn't inspect them."

Green nodded. "So what we've got to decide is whether individual shops have their own private labelling machines." He looked across at Masters. "That can't be right. There aren't enough shapes and sizes."

"That's what I thought. Their head office probably supplies one or two different models of those hand labelling gadgets and the distribution of them is haphazard. But Reed will be able to tell us."

The sergeant started to unpack his bags. "It took me some time to get on to it, Chief."

"On to what, lad?" growled Green.

"That the labels in each shop are different."

Green sat up. "They're what?"

"Look," said Reed. "I've written on every tin which branch I got it from. Look at these. Both from the Earl's Court branch. They've both got the labels with the semicircles, and both semicircles are tinged with orange paint. But the Victoria branch . . . here, take a look . . . the ends are black. And the Mile End Road is green." Reed looked across at Masters. "I began by only buying one tin at each place, Chief, but when I cottoned on that the labels were either colour-coded or different shaped, I went back and bought a second tin at each place to make sure."

"So what we're saying," said Green, "is that we can tell exactly where those tins came from."

"Where they were bought initially."

"But, Chief," protested Berger, "wouldn't Chummy have put them back in the shops he got them from? The different labels would give them away."

"They wouldn't, you know." said Reed. "I went off shopping

looking like mad for something, because I knew the Chief wouldn't send me out on a job like that unless there was something to learn. And it took me—as I said—a longish time to tumble to the fact that those labels are all different. You have to look closely, you know. Once it's been pointed out to you, there's no missing it, but I don't reckon one housewife in a thousand would notice the difference. If she did, she'd only think two girls with different machines had done the pricing."

"I'll buy that," growled Green. "We don't need telling how unobservant the general public is."

Masters faced Green. "This could help, couldn't it?"

"Me? I dunno. If all four contaminated cans come from the same shop, I could concentrate there, but there's nothing to say he doesn't live in Sheffield and slipped over to Leeds for his groceries."

"Quite. But we could ask Redcoke to inspect every strip-can and to remove any with the wrong price tags."

Green grimaced. "It might help, but there again it mightn't. I know I agreed with Reed just now, but earlier you yourself said we were dealing with a fly boy who would take good care not to have his contaminated tins examined at a check out. It could be he was careful to return them to their original shops."

"You mean I've wasted my time?" asked Reed.

"I don't think so," said Masters. "We've got to pursue this business of the labels and identify shops. Don't forget that once those patients can tell us where they bought their goods, we shall know whether our man was scrupulously careful or not. Whichever he is will help to build up his character for us."

Green said to Reed: "Nothing's ever lost or wasted in this game, lad. His Nibs has told you often enough that it all helps, even if only to eliminate somebody or to tell us one avenue of investigation is blocked to us."

Reed nodded. "Sorry I asked the question, Chief."

"There's no need to be sorry. You did well enough."

"I know, but you told us this morning we had to make a positive approach to this one. Grumbling about wasting time isn't very positive."

78

"Don't worry. You know we've got to work fast, and so the idea of wasting time is anathema. It is bound to happen while we are looking for ways of getting to grips with the problems."

"We've come a long way already, Chief," said Reed.

"That's right," added Berger. "We reckon we know the type of man we're looking for and we reckon we know how he managed to contaminate the tins. And the DCI has put out all his calls and they could bear fruit. What more could we expect in less than twenty-four hours, Chief?"

"Forget the bloke himself for a moment," said Green. "What we want to do is to stop any more innocent people being killed. Once we've done that, we'll have plenty of time to find the culprit."

"I see what you mean."

"I hope you do," said Masters, "because if we were to catch our man in half-an-hour's time, there's every possibility that more people would die and would continue to do so until all his damned tins had either been discovered or used up. He's set time bombs and it's no use our catching him and getting him to tell us where he placed them if they've already been bought and are currently residing in the larders of unsuspecting housewives."

Green sucked his teeth. "You do realise, you lads, don't you, that one or more of those tins could be in your own houses or your mothers'?"

Berger swore. "I hadn't thought of that."

"No? What does it feel like to be on a hit list?"

"Bloody frightening. And I can understand why the Chief is so worried . . . well, not worried exactly, but anxious to get all the strip-cans in every store examined or withdrawn." He looked across at Masters. "Chief, we've only to drop one unofficial word to the press and everybody—Redcokes and the DHSS—would have to toe your line."

Masters shook his head. "I can't do that, and you know it. Nor can you."

"Why not?"

"Were Redcokes to act on their own, even though they could still claim there was no absolute proof, very little harm would be done to their business, and a lot of good from the humanitarian point of view would ensue. But were we to tell the press . . . well, Redcoke would act, but they could claim they were pressurised by scandal—scandal which would cost them millions in loss of sales and loss of good-will and trust. We don't want any more disasters."

"No absolute proof, Chief? The forensic people have found the bugs in Redcoke tins. What more proof do we need?" demanded Reed.

"Quite a lot, lad," said Green. "You see, we don't think that Redcokes are responsible. We'd have to say so, wouldn't we? So Redcokes would claim that in order to solve a crime—that is, find a villain we're looking for—we took the sizeable step of ruining the reputation of one of the country's largest and most respected grocery chains. Put baldly like that, it doesn't sound like good detective work. In fact it sounds bloody stupid, and we'd have to answer for it. Not now, while the scare is on and opinion would be on our side, but in a year's time, probably, when the scare is over and people have forgotten it ever happened. Things will look different then, matey." Green thought for a moment and then continued. "Suppose, just for laughs, that it turns out that Chummy only infected four tins—the four we've already found—and we pillory Redcokes after it's all over. What's going to be said about that a year from now, in a court of law, when the Redcoke legal eagles are picking over what we are now doing and have done?" He shook his head. "His Nibs is right. This is like trying to walk on water. Unless somebody, somewhere, provides us with a raft, we're sunk."

Reed nodded to show he agreed, but was not yet ready to yield. "What about an anonymous tip to the press?"

"You weren't here," said Berger, "but Dr Moller reckons he can do that by not saying a word about Redcokes."

"How?"

"By putting the empty tins on display at the press conference tomorrow morning. Reporters and cameramen won't miss a hint like that."

"So what are we worried about?"

"I am still reluctant to do it that way," replied Masters. "What the DCI said was right. We're not out to make Redcoke suffer for this. They are a company with the highest standards of cleanliness and service, and they really are an asset to the country. I do not want to destroy them. It would be against the principles of every one of us, to make the victim pay for the culprit's misdeeds. Besides, I have a nasty suspicion that by putting Redcoke on the spot, we would be playing Chummy's game. He's out to hit them hard. I have a strong objection to helping any villain in such a fashion. If Redcoke would take the necessary steps of their own volition, with no fuss and bother, the damage would be minimal, they'd be saving lives and they'd be thwarting the madman who is trying to destroy them."

There was a moment or two of silence. The uncomfortable silence of men who are at a loss, but desperately trying to find an answer to an impossible problem.

Lake broke the silence by coming across to Masters' desk. "The file of information you asked for, sir. There's more to come, but I thought you'd like to see what we've got already."

Masters took the sheaf of medical papers and thanked Lake.

"What's that?" asked Green. "Light reading?"

Masters nodded.

"For tonight?"

"I thought I'd better look at them . . . just in case . . ."

Green got to his feet. "If you're proposing to tangle with that lot before you go to bed, it's time you were getting home to your little missus."

Reed asked, astounded, "Are you packing it in for the day, Chief?"

"What do you mean, lad?" demanded Green. "We were up all night. And because we're not sitting in this office doesn't mean we're not working."

"No . . . well . . ."

The phone rang on Masters' desk.

"It's fatal not to get away at once," counselled Green. Masters picked up the phone.

"You're right, George," said Moller without preamble. "Type

E with no salmonella or any other blessed bug means that . . . well, I don't know exactly what it means, except that our pal must have cultured his strain very carefully. He certainly didn't just half cook a pound of stewing steak and keep it warm thereafter, or he'd have had lashings of different nasties burgeoning on it. Nor did he add muck of one sort or another like Convamore suggested."

"Vegetables?"

"I think not. Vegetables—when imperfectly cooked—can produce botulism if closely sealed, but if they're left unsealed they tend to ferment in one of the usual ways—acetous, alcoholic, butyric, lactic, putrefactive and so on, and I think that this would probably kill the botulinum bugs. Certainly it would give a chance for other bugs to proliferate like hell. I'm talking about the non-lactose fermenting enterobacteriaceae like proteus, shigella and—yes— your friend salmonella. I'm not sure of all this, of course, because I doubt whether the exact parallel of our present problem has ever occurred before, and so no work will have been done on it. That means I've no references to help me, so I shall need to experiment."

"Not too fast," chided Masters. "I know you scientists! You want to get to the bottom of everything. But don't waste your time doing a lot of new experiments for me. I couldn't care less whether our man used meat or vegetable to produce his blasted brood. You've told me what I want to know, and that is that he had the ability to culture his bugs in isolation. No layman could do that. Not even by chance, I suspect?"

"George, you've opened up an avenue that I honestly don't believe anybody has ever trod before. A number of American housewives have produced botulinum from time-to-time, inadvertently, by inefficient bottling methods. A few may even have brewed one hundred per cent botulinum, but I doubt it. There are just too many bugs about wanting to get in on the act as any food hygienist will tell you."

"Thank you, Doctor."

"You make it sound as though I'd helped."

"Maybe you have."

"And maybe not. But still, it was you who opened my eyes to this complication. You're a bit of a clever bastard, aren't you, George?"

"On the quiet, yes."

Moller's voice changed. "And a good thing, too. Although they'll never know it, there may well be quite a few people alive next year at this time who would have died this year but for you."

"Thank you for the vote of confidence, but please remember we haven't got very far yet towards solving our problem."

"Yes you have, old chum. And I know. I can tell when a test is beginning to come out right. Stick to it, chum."

"Good night."

Masters put the phone down.

"Can we go now?" demanded Green, "or shall we wait for some other back-slapping stinks-man to ring up?"

"You heard some of that?"

"Didn't miss a word," replied Green, not at all abashed at confessing to eavesdropping. "And for the record, I don't reckon you're doing too badly."

"That," said Masters, "is most definitely the signal to go home. When you start throwing bouquets, it is definitely time to quit."

Chapter 5

DORIS GREEN HAD returned to her own home earlier in the day, so there was no reason why the DCI should accompany Masters who, consequently, walked home alone, clutching the file which Lake had prepared for him.

The baby was already in his cot and asleep, so Wanda was free to greet her husband and prepare him a drink to be taken in the kitchen while she put the finishing touches to supper.

"Fish, darling. Dover sole."

He grinned. "Playing safe, poppet?"

She looked up at him. Her very fair hair glinted in the rays of the westering sun coming through the window. It showed up just a trace of perspiration on her forehead, due to the non-stop domestic activity of the last two hours and the heat of the oven. "I don't think I shall open another tin until I have your assurance that it is absolutely safe to do so."

He nodded at her. "If you feel better that way . . . but I think you—and everybody else—will be safe if you avoid strip-cans."

"Strip-cans?"

"The ones you open with a key."

"They are the dangerous ones?"

"All four of the outbreaks . . ."

"Four?"

"There's been another. In Bournemouth."

"Could it . . . grow worse? Spread?"

"It wouldn't spread like an epidemic, but there could easily be more cases."

She came and stood close to him. "I heard a man on television . . ."

"Cutton?"

"Was that his name? I didn't understand him. He pretended there was no danger. Nothing to worry about."

"There isn't—for you, if you take care and avoid strip-cans."

"Why couldn't he have said that? I trust you implicitly, so I know for certain that what you have told me is true. Why can't everybody be given the same advice?"

Masters kissed her forehead. "Because the reaction of many people would not be the same as yours, my darling. It is feared that if strip-cans were to be mentioned specifically, thousands of people who had just eaten from them would immediately begin to suffer from bogus, autosuggestive symptoms and would swamp every doctor and hospital in the country. And they would have to be taken seriously because among them there could be genuine cases."

"That sounds reasonable," replied Wanda, "but it does seem a pity nothing can be done to prevent further trouble."

He grinned at her. "We're doing our best."

"I know that, you chump. And I know you'll not stop until you've put it right. You won't, will you?"

He shook his head and then said: "I'm rather pleased you're urging me on. Now you won't be able to complain because I've brought a file of work home . . ."

She pushed away from him. "You big . . . I could wallop you . . . and you're looking tired."

"I'll manage. Having you here chases it all away . . . tiredness, trouble . . ." He took her in his arms. "You're the complete restorative. The elixir man has sought in vain down the ages."

"Rubbish. But nice rubbish. Now, if you'll let me go, I can do something about the Dover sole . . ."

It was a pleasant, companionable evening in the little house. The sky had clouded over, so that Masters needed a lamp to read by. Wanda sat in the huge chair opposite but, because of the size of the room, she was very close to him. She read, too, her latest library book, Marguerite Yourcenar's *Memoirs of Hadrian*. She looked up once and caught his eye, when the first splashes of rain hit the windows.

"Cosy," she murmured with a smile. It was the only word she spoke, though after getting up to go upstairs to see their child was still sleeping, undisturbed by the rain, she prepared her husband a drink and set it down on the small pie-crust table on which his ashtray stood.

He grunted his thanks, aware of her gesture, but too totally immersed in his work to pay her undivided attention. It was more than half an hour later when he leaned back, leaving the open file on his knees.

"The fish . . ." he began.

"For supper? The Dover sole?"

"Why fish and not meat?"

"We had a joint last night, remember. We can't afford joints every night. Nobody can."

He looked across at her. "I would have thought Dover sole would have been as dear as meat. Dearer than, say, liver and bacon or a savoury mince."

She nodded. "They were a bit of an extravagance, perhaps."

"But you provided them because I like them so much?"

She blushed. "Why not?"

"No reason why not, my sweet. It was very thoughtful of you."

"And they don't come in tins," she added sombrely.

"Ah!"

"What does that mean?" Now there was a hint of alarm in her voice.

"Only that they come out of the sea."

"Of course they do. They're built for it . . . oh, my God!" She put one slim hand to her mouth and her eyes widened in horror. "Don't tell me those bacteria infest the seas, too."

He stretched across and took her hands in his. "Don't get alarmed, my beautiful. Convamore and Moller told us that all the outbreaks have been caused by type E botulinum. They also told us that though that type is rare in Britain, it is nevertheless peculiar to the northern hemisphere. Not knowing much about these things, I took that to mean that they inhabit the land surfaces."

"But they don't just do that? They get into water as well—lakes and rivers and seas?"

"Apparently." He tapped the file. "One of these papers says that type E is predominantly found in the *waters* of the northern hemisphere, and carries on to say that one of its distinctive features is that it can grow and produce its toxin at four degrees centigrade—the temperature of a domestic refrigerator."

"Is that knowledge important?"

"Important to the case? That would be hard to say, but it's an important lesson to me."

"In what way?"

"Not just to presume I understand what experts mean. Convamore and Moller were, strictly speaking, correct to say that type E is found mostly in the northern hemisphere, but I should not have assumed they meant only the land masses. I should have asked questions."

"They were talking to laymen. They could have said they meant the oceans as well as the land."

"True. But egg-heads often lose sight of the fact that because they know what they are talking about, others don't, necessarily."

Wanda took her hands from his and pushed back a strand of hair that had fallen over her eyes. "It stands to reason, though, doesn't it, that streams and rivers will carry the bacteria from the land down to the water?"

He nodded. "Now we know, yes, it is logical."

"You're a very clever detective man to have those papers gathered together so that you could read it all up for yourself."

"Clever . . . but worried."

"Nonsense, darling. Knowledge is . . ." Once again she stopped in alarm. "Oh, no! Don't tell me they contaminate fish?"

"As to that—whether they contaminate wet fish in any way, I can't say. I don't think they do, because we were told they contaminate only dead flesh. But this man I've been reading is insistent on mentioning fish. In one place he says that types A and B are characteristically contaminants of meat and vegetables, type E of fish. Then later on he says, in context, that certain fish dishes which have caused outbreaks abroad were contaminated with type E of the organism, which is particularly associated with fish."

"That raises at least two points," said Wanda slowly.

He waited for her to continue.

"What does he mean by characteristically? Absolutely distinctive?"

"I think not. He must mean likely. Typical perhaps. But not absolute, because don't forget that he went on to use the phrase 'particularly associated' which suggests that it doesn't go for fish and fish alone. And that must be true, because both Convamore and Moller have cultured type E from cans of meat of various kinds."

"We seem to have resolved that point. And you know what the second one is, don't you?"

"You are saying that the chances are that the botulinum bacteria that have been used in all these tins came originally from a tin of fish."

"Don't you think so?"

"Of course I do. Now I've read these papers, I'd bet on it. And fish comes in strip-cans—sardines, herrings, mackerel . . ."

"I've got a strip-can of cod's roe in my pantry."

"There you are then, my poppet—a working conclusion at last."

"Is it going to help?" she asked in amazement. "How on earth can the fact that the horrible person who is causing all this trouble started it in a tin of fish be going to help you solve this crime?"

"It's not only that . . ." began Masters. The telephone interrupted him before he could complete the sentence.

"Who can that be at this time of night?" asked Wanda, a little irritated by the intrusion.

Masters got to his feet. "There's only one way to find out, my sweet."

"George?"

"Yes, it's me. What's up, Bill?"

"My missus connived with yours before she left your house today."

"What about?"

88

"Food. What they were going to give us to eat."

"Oh, yes? You had fish, too, did you?"

"I did."

"And you ate it?"

"Lapped it up."

"But something is worrying you?"

Green's voice was more sombre than usual as he replied.

"My trouble is I've got a long memory, George. I can remember reading that the outbreak of botulism in Brum in seventy-eight was caused by salmon canned in Alaska."

"True. Did you recall that before or after you ate supper?"

"After."

"And that is causing you to feel a bit queasy?"

Green snorted. "I've been married the best part of thirty years, and nothing Doris has cooked in all that time has ever upset me."

"I'm sure. But the thought of botulism and fish . . .?"

"No. Nothing like that. I called because I thought it might help you if I reminded you fish could be implicated even though we haven't come across it in any of the four outbreaks. I don't know what lines you're thinking along, or what all that bumf you took home tonight is telling you—if anything—but I thought that if you had fish to take into consideration as well, it might help to solve some problem or spark some idea."

Masters didn't reply for a moment or two. The silence was, in fact, so prolonged that Green demanded to know if his colleague was still listening.

"Listening?" asked Masters. "Listening, Bill, and thinking furiously."

"About what I've said?"

"Just that, chum."

"You mean it's of some use?"

"Invaluable—probably."

"Probably? In what way?"

"Steady on. I'm thinking it through."

"Thinking what through?"

Masters grimaced at Wanda, who had joined him in the hall, and then replied. "Well, Bill, suppose the whole thing started in a contaminated tin of fish—like the Alaskan salmon you've just reminded me about—and our man recognised it, it would mean that he would have his bacteria ready-made. And that overcomes the problem of how he could have cultured it without producing other nasties like salmonella at the same time."

"He'd have to be a bit of a scientific wizard to recognise it, wouldn't he?"

"Of course. But that only confirms our belief that the chap we are looking for is a pretty high-powered boffin."

"He'd have to be more high-powered to recognise it than to culture it. After all, American housewives culture it every year without thinking about it."

"True enough. Our own people ought to be able to tell us how it could be recognised, and who would be likely to do so."

Green grunted sceptically.

"You don't think so? Ah, well, that's what sprang to my mind when you mentioned fish. Perhaps by tomorrow I might have some other thoughts about it. Thank you for ringing, Bill."

"So long. Don't work too hard."

As Masters put the phone down, Wanda said: "You old fraud, George. You let Bill think that the fish idea had not occurred to you before he rang."

"Why not, my sweet? It will encourage him to let him think he was first with the news. If I'd said that I had travelled along that particular road before he rang, it would either have dampened his enthusiasm or—worse—he could have disbelieved me, thinking I was trying to hog all the credit for myself."

"Surely not? Not Bill?"

Masters grinned. "He's human, poppet. We all like our ideas to be first and best."

"In that case, why did you let him think he was teaching you something? You're human, too."

"We're both on the same side," he said simply.

She came across to him and perched on his knee like a child. With her arms round his neck, she clung to him, giving physical, tactile approval of his attitude.

After a moment or two—

"Are you going to do any more reading tonight?"

"Not reading," he said enigmatically, but the words were not so allusive as to obscure their hidden meaning from her. She smiled contentedly.

Everybody was early in the office the next morning. Thankfully, Masters realised that the sense of urgency he had tried to inspire was now pervading all their minds, including those of Lake and his two helpers who had, he learned, kept a night-long watch between them.

"Thought any more about the fish, George?" asked Green.

Masters nodded.

"Come on then. Out with it."

"Out with what?"

"Your conclusions, mate."

"I didn't say I'd reached any conclusions. I just said I'd thought about fish. So much so that you gave me a virtually sleepless night."

"Come off it."

Masters took out his pipe and tin of Warlock Flake.

"I'm not joking, Bill."

"You are, you know," replied Green. "Somewhere along the line you are. You may have had a sleepless night. But if you did, you'll have reached some conclusions, because you simply do not think for hours on end without producing some result. So which is false? The claim to have had a sleepless night or the claim that you reached no conclusion?"

Berger and Reed seemed to be waiting for his reply as anxiously as Green. Masters filled his pipe slowly. At last—

"Bill, what I was most concerned about was something you said."

"About the fish?"

"Not that. Yesterday afternoon you said that a countrywide search for somebody with a grievance against Redcoke was not our scene."

"Right. It isn't. But if we have to we'll do it."

"It'll take a long time though," added Reed.

Masters nodded. "Too long. And without any guarantee of success in the end. But it is what is expected of us—hence this Incident Centre and the steps we have taken so far. Even if we fail, we'll have done the job the right way and nobody will be able to fault us."

"Hang on, hang on," said Green. "George, you've been trumpeting on about not thinking of failure, and here you are now, introducing it as if it were a distinct possibility."

"True."

"After less than forty-eight hours."

"True again."

Green looked at him closely. "George, you're being too smooth. Too easy by half. You're up to something, you old bastard. I know you are."

"If I am, it's only because you encouraged me. After you said this sort of investigation was not our scene, you urged me to revert to our usual method of working. You actually said . . ."

"I remember. I said that you are a fast worker and you should give us something else—some other way of finding a solution." Green eyed him shrewdly. "That's what you've been working on. You lost your sleep over trying to find an alternative approach."

"Yes."

"And?"

"What would you say to trying a long shot?"

"How long?"

"As long as they come."

Masters was conscious of the fact that his words had caused a stir of expectancy. Reed and Berger were watching him intently, tensely, as though afraid to speak lest this faint chance should take fright and disappear again for ever. Green was eyeing him shrewdly: weighing the matter up as nearly as he could with so little to go on.

"We drop everything for it?" asked Green at last.

"No. We do what we have to do this morning. Then this afternoon we try the long shot."

"Right. What is it?"

"Do you mind if . . . look, Bill, I don't want to hold back, but I don't want to go off at half-cock either. I haven't got it completely worked out. As a matter of fact, I did stay awake a long time, with no conclusions, as I told you. I had given up the struggle and was just dropping off when this glimmer of an idea came to me. I think I felt so satisfied—mentally—that something should at last have appeared over the horizon that my mind gasped with relief and I fell asleep without working things out. I must do that before we can act on it. Can I leave it there?"

Green shrugged. "If you're sure you remembered what it was. Ideas that come just as you're falling asleep have a happy knack of disappearing before morning."

"I remember it. I grabbed it firmly by the tail to prevent it popping back into its hole."

"In that case . . ."

"Thanks. Reed, we shall need the car for this afternoon and our overnight bags."

"We're travelling, Chief?"

"We're travelling. Now back to routine. Berger, you help Inspector Lake to collate any replies that have arrived in answer to the DCI's enquiries. Reed, you bring your bags of tins and accompany the DCI and myself to Messrs Redcoke. We're going to appeal to reason, and we've got to get a bit of co-operation before Dr Moller holds his eleven o'clock press conference."

They got to their feet as Lake came across to them. "A message has just come in from Taunton, sir. Mr Burnham died in the night."

"Thank you. That's the father and younger child. Any word of the mother and elder child?"

"They are both gravely ill, sir. Everybody else—those in Derby, Colchester and Bournemouth—is still alive, and all three hospitals are hopeful that they can save them all."

"Thank heaven for that."

"I've always said you have the luck of the devil, George," said Green heavily.

"You usually put it slightly differently," retorted Masters. "As I recall, you invariably refer to me as a jammy bastard."

"No matter. Whichever it is, the luck or the jam had better be

93

spread pretty thick on this idea of yours, because when I think of some nutter going around killing whole families, I begin to get a bit restive. As it is, when we find him, I don't reckon I'll be able to keep my hands off him."

Masters didn't reply, and they left the office.

The Redcoke head office was one of those buildings of which the original Georgian façade had been preserved, while everything behind the front wall had been rebuilt in the modern egg-box style.

Masters, Green and Reed made their way up the two old stone steps to the huge wooden door, double-leaved with great brass knobs centrally placed on each half. The glass screen door was manned by a female commissionaire: an efficient, well-spoken woman, dressed—though not looking like—an air hostess in out-door suit and hat. Her face—as Green later described it—reminded him of a photograph he had once seen of an ace Russian shot-putter, supposedly female.

"Have you an appointment with the Managing Director?"

"No, but this is extremely urgent. There has been no time to make an appointment."

"I will ask his personal assistant if she will see you." The attitude was not one which endeared itself to Masters, and when they were met on the third floor by the PA, another middle-aged woman of forbidding mien, he was rather taken aback, but she led them promptly to the office of the Managing Director.

"Mr Stratton, these are the . . . er . . . men who demanded to see you."

Green hung back as Masters walked in. "Gentlemen, darling," said Green to the PA. "If we weren't, I'd be making rude remarks about your face reminding me of one I once saw on a girl who was walking about as if she had an open safety pin in the seat of her knickers. It hurt me to look at *her* phisog, too."

By the time Green had carefully shut the door in the face of the outraged PA, Masters was shaking hands with Stratton.

"I'm a busy man, Chief Superintendent."

"So am I, sir."

Stratton gestured towards chairs and then asked: "What's it all about?"

"You mean you don't know, sir?"

"Have I done something criminal?"

"You have heard that there have been four outbreaks of botulism?"

"Yes, I'd heard there was a scare. Four cases, you say?"

"Four outbreaks, sir, twenty or more cases, and so far two deaths."

Stratton held up both hands. "Please, Chief Superintendent, get to the point. What has this to do with me?"

Masters said heavily: "They had all eaten products bought in your shops and our forensic people have recovered all the tins and have cultured botulism from scrapings taken from them."

Stratton sat motionless for a moment.

"Nonsense," he stuttered at last. "Absolute nonsense. This is defamatory."

"Do you really think," asked Masters quietly, "that I would be wasting my time here if what I have said is not true?"

"But . . . but it is impossible. Our standards of hygiene . . ."

"Let us clear the decks," interrupted Masters. "I have the greatest admiration for your shops and your hygiene and your marketing activities. That is why I am here, now, instead of applying for an injunction to close you down."

"Close me down? Close nearly two hundred shops and supermarkets? You'd never get an injunction."

Masters nodded. "If the High Court didn't close you, the public would, Mr Stratton—once the knowledge was out. And let me assure you that the peccant tins—with your price labels on them— are sitting on a bench at the forensic laboratory, waiting to be displayed at a press conference at eleven o'clock this morning. We won't even have to mention the name Redcoke. The photographers will do it all for us, unless I ask for the tins to be kept under wraps."

Stratton considered this for a moment and then got to his feet. It seemed as though the action made him a different man.

"Right," he said incisively. "What you've said has shocked me.

Now we've got to decide what to do. And quickly. Two people dead! Whether they are dead from eating Redcoke products or not is immaterial if you think they are." He swung round on Masters. "What have we to do?"

"First off," said Masters, liking this new man, "we must ensure that Redcoke is not harmed in any way if we can avoid it. We all regard your stores as a national asset and we have no desire to call them into disrepute."

"Thank God for that."

"To this end, can DCI Green use your phone to call Dr Moller at the forensic laboratory, to tell him to get the cans out of sight before the press starts to arrive?"

"Of course."

"How secure is it? I don't want some telephonist to get a hint . . ."

"There's a call box—one of those bubble things fastened to the wall—on the next floor down. It is a direct phone—bypasses the house exchange—here. I've got some coins."

"Ta," said Green, accepting some two-pence pieces. "Will Miss Scratch-me-backside outside mind showing me where to go?"

Stratton touched a button. "Nora, Mr Green is coming out to use the coin-box phone. Please show him where it is."

"Now," said Masters when Green had gone, "I believe somebody is trying to work off a grudge against Redcoke by implicating your shops in these outbreaks."

"You mean some crack-brained bastard is killing people off to ease a grudge against Redcoke?"

"Yes."

"How?"

"By impregnating the contents of tins of food bought in your shops—and then returning them to the shelves."

"He's doing it in the shops?"

"I think not. It's a laboratory job. He buys tins, takes them home, doctors them and then takes them back—probably to different branches—for some unsuspecting shopper to buy."

"Indiscriminately?"

96

"Absolutely—or so we believe, and we base that on the knowledge that contaminated tins have been bought in four of your widely-separated branches."

"So there may be poisoned tins in a hundred shops! We could never deal with that. There must be at the very least over a hundred thousand tins on display at any given moment in our bigger outlets."

"Quite. The problem is vast. But we have been working on it for a day and a half now. Certain things have emerged. The most significant from your point of view is that the murderer appears to be using—exclusively—cans of meat or fish that are opened with keys. Strip-cans, but not those you pull the lid off with a lifting ring."

Stratton eyed him. "You're sure of this?"

"As far as we know at the moment."

"Because all the tins you've got are of that type? Not much to go on is it? Four tins?"

"Not a big sample, to be sure. But we and the forensic scientists believe we know the method that is being used to pierce and reseal the cans. It's a tricky job, and has to be done in the absence of oxygen or air. Why, doesn't matter. What is important is that the injecting has to be done at a weak spot in the can . . ."

"Where it is half-scored through so that it tears easily?"

"Exactly. And also where it can be hidden from view. That is, under the flap which takes the key."

Stratton sat back. "He must know what he's about."

"He does."

"At any rate you seem to have rumbled the method."

"We hope so. Forensic have been trying to copy it. They are getting about ten per cent success."

"You mean . . . you mean that if the bastard bought a hundred tins he'd only contaminate ten of them successfully?"

"Only, sir?" asked Reed.

"Sorry. But you must agree that for nine out of ten to fail is better than . . ."

"It is, sir. But we've only located four."

Masters interrupted. "Now, Mr Stratton, would it be possible to

97

empty your shelves—everywhere—of those items that are opened with keys?"

"It's got to be." He pressed another button on his intercom.

"Fenton."

"Reggie, what do we sell at the moment in cans that are supplied with keys and which strip open on a ribbon of metal. Disregard ring pulls."

"Not a lot of varieties, sir, but a hell of a lot of volume."

"What?"

"Corned beef, large and small. Two or three types of luncheon meat. Ham. Mackerel fillets, cod roes, soft-herring roes, sardines. No others spring to mind except some tins of nuts."

"Thanks. Come in here straight away, Reggie."

Stratton turned to Masters. "We'll remove them all."

"Thank you. I don't think they'll be lost. Either we can examine them or—when we catch our man—we can make him tell us where he placed the contaminated cans."

"Hm-m."

The door opened and Reggie came in. Behind him came Green.

"All fixed?" asked Masters.

Green nodded.

"Reggie," said Stratton, wasting no time in introducing the young executive type. "Phone every area manager and speak to him personally. If by some mischance he is absent, speak to his deputy. Leave no doubt in their minds about this. They are personally to instruct every manager—immediately—that every can of goods that is supplied with, and opened by a key—excluding ring pulls—is to be removed from the shelves before twelve o'clock today. Each manager is to supervise the operation personally, and will not delegate it. Each manager will report personally, by phone, to his area manager, that these orders have been carried out to the letter. Area managers will then phone you to tell you the job has been completed. You, in turn, will report completion to me, here, by twelve-thirty. Is that clear?"

"Yes, sir. Absolutely."

"This afternoon, area managers will visit each shop in person to see for himself that the job has been done, and will certify in writing that they have done so. The certificates will be expressed to reach here tomorrow morning. All this to be done without fuss and without explanation. Understand? As secretly as possible."

"Right, sir. Got it."

"Away you go, then."

As Reggie turned to leave, Green said: "And, lad, tell them to make sure none of that type of tin is lurking anywhere else where an odd shopper might find it—behind an upright or another stack of tins."

Reggie nodded.

"Add, please," said Masters, "that all those tins should immediately be put under lock and key."

"Heavens, yes," said Stratton. "I'd forgotten that. They are to be put where nobody can get at them. In the manager's office if needs be. We have the odd light-fingered employee. Bound to have among the number we employ."

"Can the shelves be refilled, sir?"

"Not with similar cans, Reggie. Tell them to put sugar or tea or bottled coffee in the gaps."

"Right, sir."

When Reggie had gone, Stratton said: "There's not much more I can do. If adulterated cans have already been sold . . . that's beyond my powers."

"You've acted courageously and promptly," said Masters.

"Can we warn people?"

Masters shook his head. "Against all those products? Ham, luncheon meat . . . anything may be implicated. I've been into all this with the health authorities, Mr Stratton. They believe that such a warning would cause a panic and a consequent breakdown of medical services. Besides, my colleagues and I are extremely anxious not to mention the name of Redcoke. We have no wish to damage the reputation of what is, after all, a national institution that is of benefit one way or another to every member of the community."

"Thank you."

"Besides our personal views," continued Masters, "I have a professional antipathy to doing the criminal's work for him."

"How do you mean?"

"I believe the reason for what he is doing is to harm Redcoke. I'm not prepared to help him achieve his aim by crucifying you."

"Thank you, again. May I be allowed to say that such an attitude does a lot to dispel the despair and anger I am feeling at this news you have brought."

"I'm sorry to have sprung it on you, sir, but I didn't realise that you had not been told that your goods were implicated."

"Stands to reason, though, doesn't it?" said Green. "I came here yesterday to ask about your new buildings, Mr Stratton, but I didn't tell your property office why I was asking. There was no reason why I should. And I can't see the DHSS getting in touch with you. They would expect the Home Office to do it and as they've handed the investigation over to us, they would naturally assume it was our job. Too many cooks passing the buck, that's the trouble."

Stratton nodded. "And everybody trying to keep their counsel. I'm grateful for that, so I can't complain." He touched the intercom. "Nora, coffee for four please. Lots of it." He looked across at Masters. "I assume you can stay for coffee?"

"That's very kind of you. We'd like coffee, and we have a few more questions for you."

"Oh, yes?"

"Not to safeguard your customers. More to help our enquiries. You've probably noticed that Sergeant Reed has a couple of plastic carriers."

"I wondered about those."

"They're filled with goods from your shops. No, not suspected tins. We bought them for a comparison of price labels."

"I know very little about . . ."

He was interrupted by his PA opening the door and edging a trolley into the office. "I had the restaurant send up biscuits and a variety of cakes, Mr Stratton."

"Thank you, Nora. Would you pour out for us. I never know quite how to operate those push-button thermos jugs."

"They're quite easy, sir, as long as you remember to hold the cup under the spout and not to try to do it with a saucer."

"I see. Thank you."

As the elevenses were handed round, Stratton made another call on his intercom. "Peter, I've a question about price labelling. Come in, will you? Now?" He turned to Masters. "We might as well have the expert in from the outset. Peter Musgrove is our equipment buyer. He's been with us since the year dot and knows everything about everything to do with cash registers, shelving, labelling guns, scales, meat saws, etcetera, etcetera."

"He's the chap I want to see then," said Reed, taking over as if in order to show Masters that the enthusiasm engendered by the pep-talk of the previous day had not waned. "I'll just finish this coffee . . ."

"Thank you, Nora." Stratton dismissed his PA and turned to Reed. "You're the one who went on the shopping spree, are you?"

"Yes, sir."

"Who pays when you have to go out and spend money like that?"

"You do, sir. We all do. Public funds foot the bill, though it comes out of the police entitlement, so we're not allowed to go over the top."

"I see."

Peter Musgrove knocked and entered. Masters was slightly shocked by his appearance because he was exactly like the picture of the man he had envisaged from Stratton's brief description of him. He was a small man of about sixty with a head of grey, closely curled hair. He wore an impeccable mid-grey suit, white shirt and club tie, and no doubt had been accustomed to doing so for many years. And yet he looked ill-at-ease in them: as though he had suddenly been promoted to executive level from a supermarket floor and had bought a new rig-out to mark the occasion. Very different from Reggie, who had given the impression that a business suit was the only wear and a smart young man's first duty was to sign an annual contract with a weekly valetting firm.

"Peter, these gentlemen from Scotland Yard are investigating an extremely serious crime which, they believe, involves . . . well, I don't quite know what it involves, but something to do with our price labels, I believe."

"They haven't recovered that container load of dry goods that was hijacked, have they, John?" asked Musgrove.

Masters was surprised that Musgrove addressed the Managing Director by his first name. It somehow seemed out of place: too modern an approach for an old-worldly employee.

"Nothing like that, Peter." Stratton turned to Reed. "I believe you said this was your part of the enquiry."

Reed nodded. "Do you mind if I lay these out on your desk, sir?" As he spoke, the sergeant began lining up the tins so that the small price tags showed. He turned to Musgrove. "See these? Different sizes, different shapes, different tips of colour on some of them."

Musgrove peered. "Yes, indeed. They have."

"Okay. I've got some tins of your stuff I'm interested in and I want to know exactly where they come from."

"Oh, yes?"

"So, have you got a list of which of your shops uses different shapes or colour codes?"

"No, no. Of course not."

"Sure, Peter?" asked Stratton.

"Absolutely. I just buy labelling guns as and when we need them. We've been supplying them to our outlets now for close on twenty-five years, and in that time there have been many patterns from different manufacturers."

"And you send them out willy-nilly?" asked Reed, disappointed.

"Of course we do. If a supermarket with twenty guns has one go wrong, we don't withdraw the other nineteen. We send a replacement from whatever we've got. And we don't keep big stocks. Just two or three at any time. It may be a different size and type altogether from the others."

"And the labels themselves?"

"They're all coded by the manufacturers. Each shop puts in a requisition for the codes it needs. At the moment we're just beginning to introduce new guns. They'll save time because they'll do a row of cans all at once. You just draw it across each layer while it's still in the outer or—if you like—once they're lined up on display. But they're going out gradually—as replacements—and even then not on a one for one basis. We've a lot of money tied up in things like price guns. And before we know where we are we shall be using these new computer symbols, and they will be even more expensive to install, though I think they'll stop mistakes at tills."

"And these faint colours at the ends of the labels?"

"Meaningless. I don't know how they get there. The manufacturers may be able to tell you, but we certainly don't waste time and money in colour-coding price tags."

"Pity," said Reed. He looked across at Masters. "It would be no use asking for samples of labels from every shop, Chief, because the chances are they've all got the same colours if the distribution is haphazard."

Masters nodded his agreement.

"Is that all, Sergeant?" asked Stratton.

"Yes, thank you, sir." Reed began to repack his groceries. Masters got to his feet. "We shall be in touch again, Mr Stratton. Next time I'll try to warn you of our arrival so that the female dragon at your door doesn't start breathing fire."

"Who? Nora?"

"The female commissionaire."

"Lucinda! Peter, here, calls her Frau Krautworst, which he tells me is a good old German name, but which sounds a bit like Cabbage Sausage to me."

Green looked across at Musgrove. "I reckon you and me think alike, mate. I'd got Katzenjammer in mind—from the old cartoons, you know."

As Masters was leaving, he said to Stratton: "There is just one more thing, suggested by the pathologist. I don't think we need to worry our heads about it at the moment, but he quite rightly suggested that we should investigate whether all the contaminated tins passed through the same warehouse."

"The suggestion being that one of our distributing depots is infected with botulism?"

"We have to try to think of every eventuality. I personally discount that particular one on many grounds, not the least of which is your recognised high regard for cleanliness and hygiene. That is why I said we wouldn't worry about it unless and until there are some indications which make it seem necessary."

"Thank you. I must say the attitude you are adopting over this business puts Redcoke in your debt. It would be so easy for you to fling mud."

Masters grinned. "If I were to do that I'd never hear the last of it. My wife is one of your very satisfied customers. If I were to jeopardise her marketing . . ."

Stratton smiled. "And I am supposed to attribute your natural courtesy and concern entirely to Mrs Masters' shopping habits?"

"It's as good a reason as any. There's very little she does which does not find favour in my eyes."

"Then, in addition to everything else, you're a very lucky man, Chief Superintendent. If you ever feel like retiring from Scotland Yard, let me know, will you. I'd be grateful for the chance . . ."

Masters held up one hand. "Please leave it unsaid, Mr Stratton. I'll see you again, no doubt."

"What happens now?" asked Green as Reed drove them back to the Yard.

"See how Berger is getting on with reports from the various police authorities. If it looks as though he is getting no joy at all, instruct Keith Lake to deal with them from now on."

"And if Berger is getting some leads?"

"Issue another instruction to the forces concerned. Ask them to investigate the background of every person affected by the Redcoke property deals, with a view to locating somebody, not too distantly connected with them, who is a scientist, technician, lab assistant or in any way connected with science and technology. We'd like details of employment and places of work etcetera, so that we can start investigating."

Green nodded. "That's going to cut it down to size. There won't be many."

"If any."

"Whichever, it will at least be a manageable number."

"Even if there's nobody?" asked Reed.

"Yes, lad. When I was at school, we used to have to learn poetry by heart, not like now when kids don't have to learn anything."

"What's that got to do with it?"

"We had to learn chunks by a chap called Yeats who wrote 'The Lake Isle of Innisfree'. One bit, I remember, was that nobody gets old and crafty and wise. So if nobody gets old and crafty and wise, he's not going to be much of a stumbling block for us, and if nobody's not going to be a stumbling block, he's going to be manageable."

Green glanced at Masters as though inviting approbation for this blatant elision. Reed muttered: "Good God," while Masters laughed aloud.

"What's up?" asked Green blandly. "You're always saying that nobody must ever be disregarded, and my old mum was always saying that Mr Nobody broke more cups and saucers in our house than anybody else. So if he can break pots we ought to be able to nick him for it."

"Sorry I started this, Chief," said Reed.

"I wouldn't have missed it for worlds. I was anticipating a few words on nobody's business being everybody's business."

"Rubbish," said Green. "You're misquoting."

"*I'm* misquoting?"

"Yes," replied Green airily. "It's unfair to try to make points by misquoting. What you should have said is 'everybody's business is nobody's business', and that doesn't fit our present case at all."

The car drew into the Yard car park and ended the chatter which, Masters realised, had been Green's contribution towards keeping the party cheerful.

As they reached his office, Masters remarked that while Green and Reed were attending to the tasks already discussed, he would report to Anderson. "He'll expect me to tell him where we've got to, and he'll be pleased to hear that Redcoke has been so co-operative."

Green grunted. "He'll be pleased enough—on the basis that half a loaf is better than no bread."

"The removal of the tins still in the shops does not warn or protect the customers who may have already bought infected ones."

Green nodded.

"It's as far as I dare go, Bill. I was ordered not to start a panic."

"Right. And Stratton couldn't have done more than he did. Nevertheless, it leaves me with a nasty taste in my mouth."

"Let's see if we can remove it," said Masters. "It's still quite early. If Anderson doesn't keep me too long and you can get your bits and pieces sorted, we could be on our way well before lunch."

Green, who, Masters knew, was bursting with curiosity as to their destination, made no attempt to ask where they were going. In fairness, Masters decided he had better tell the older man.

"We'll be visiting the Isle of Wight, Bill."

Green still held back his curiosity. His only remark was: "It's high summer. We're going to have a job getting a bed in any sort of decent pub."

"Use your influence, Bill."

"My influence?"

"You've always told me that you and Doris go there every year. You must be well known in the hotel you usually patronise. Ring them and say it's vital."

"The missus and I always stay at the Trust House in Ryde. Yelf's Hotel."

"Fine. See what you can do for us. Just for one night. Two at the most."

"You'll be lucky."

"We could split up—two and two—if necessary."

"Anything you say. Then I'll ring Doris and ask her to bring my sandshoes over."

"Tell the others to let their people know we'll be away tonight. I'll ring Wanda after I've seen Anderson."

The Assistant Commissioner listened to his report and then said to Masters: "This long shot of yours, George. You haven't told me anything about it, and I'm not asking you to do so at this stage, but I would like to know how confident you feel about it."

"I can't claim to have a great deal of confidence in the idea itself, sir."

"Yet you're taking your whole team off the case here."

"I am, sir, because I really am confident that I've got to break out of the routine here. We've gone a long way with it, but getting Stratton's co-operation was, quite honestly, the last positive step I could think of. The alternative is to stay where we are and wait for something to break. I daren't do that. I've got to pursue the investigation actively, otherwise we are going to stagnate and more people are going to be ill and perhaps die . . ."

"Hold it, George. The same number will become ill and die whether you go or not, now Stratton has removed the tins from his shelves. We can't warn people who have already bought contaminated produce."

"With respect, sir. I hope that's not true. If I can lay my hands on the culprit and make him tell me in which branches he deposited his blasted doctored cans . . .

"Then we can put out a limited warning, you mean?"

"Why not, sir?"

Anderson nodded. "There can be no objections when there's no longer any speculation. Get after your man, George. And the best of luck."

As the large Rover sped westwards, making for Southampton and the Cowes car ferry, Masters turned to Green who was sitting, as was his habit, in the nearside back seat which he considered to be the safest spot in the car.

"Explanation time, Bill."

"Don't rush it," said Green airily. "There's no great reason why Reed and Berger and I should know why we're going to the Izzly of Widgett. After all, it's a nice day in July, and a trip to the seaside makes a nice break from routine and the heat and noise of London. You can keep us in the dark . . ."

"On a nice day in July?"

"Figuratively speaking. You can keep us in the dark for as long as you like. After all, why spoil a nice outing like this with thoughts of the nastiest crime we've encountered in Britain since the late Jack the Ripper roamed the gaslit streets of the metropolis?"

"Have you finished, Bill?"

"Don't stop him, Chief," implored Berger. "He's getting quite lyrical."

"That's right, Chief," added Reed who was driving. "After all, it's not much more than an hour ago that he was giving us a load of bull about 'The Lake Isle of Innisfree' and Mister Nobody. So what's he got to complain about if you mention the Isle of Wight and Mister No Reason."

Green growled. "Cut it out, you two comedians. You're both dying with curiosity. I can tell because all four of your ears have grown big and red . . ."

Reed joined the motorway, the worst time for Green with his fear of speed and traffic. Masters hastened to take his colleague's mind off the great juggernauts that were pounding along all about them.

"Bill," he said. "When I said I wanted somewhere quiet but pleasant to take Wanda for a few days' holiday before Michael was born . . ."

"Michael William," corrected Green, hanging on to the back of Berger's seat.

"Sorry. Michael William. At that time you and Doris recommended the Isle of Wight. I'd never been there, but you were familiar with it and so fond of it that you paid it regular visits every summer."

"What's up?" queried Green. "Didn't it come up to expectations?"

"Very much so. It was ideal there in the spring. Clean, pleasant, quiet, refreshing . . . Wanda and I told you how much we'd enjoyed it."

Green grunted in confirmation. The knuckles of his hands were white with the intensity of his grip.

"Slow down a bit, Reed. I can't concentrate on what I want to say at this speed."

"Sorry, Chief."

Masters turned again to Green. "What we didn't tell you, Bill, was that on our last morning there we had just a momentary unpleasant clash with a member of the local police."

"You what?" demanded Green, apparently forgetting his fear of speed in the anger he experienced at the thought of Wanda being upset or inconvenienced. "Why didn't you tell us?"

"Because it wasn't important and, as I said, it was a momentary incident which I dealt with quite easily."

"I'll bet," murmured Berger.

"What happened?" demanded Green.

"Each morning we were there, we took a gentle stroll along the beach at Shanklin. The weather was blustery, but there were few people about and the wind and waves provided us with a lot of interest. Wanda enjoyed herself. She collected smooth pebbles and pretty shells . . ."

"And you played ducks and drakes with flat stones," interjected Green. "I know. It's about par for the course."

"Maybe. But whatever it was, Wanda and I came to value those excursions. She was very fit, as you know, despite the imminence of the young man's birth, and she felt that stooping to pick up shells was useful exercise, and the wind put colour into her cheeks . . ."

"Now who's being lyrical?"

"Anyway, you can imagine my attitude when, on the last morning we were there, we had just got down to the beach when a local bluebottle somewhat brusquely ordered us off the sand and forbade us the promenade, too."

"He what? You're joking, Chief."

"I assure you I'm not. What was worse, however, was that the bobby refused us an explanation. He merely said we had got there before the road blocks had been erected and now we must go back beyond them."

Green snorted. "Without giving a reason?"

"That's what got my goat. That and the fact that he was much less than courteous to us."

"Until you revealed who you were, I suppose?"

"Quite."

"You made him regret his attitude, I hope?"

"With Wanda present?"

"I see what you mean. Lucky for him. But you did get to know why they were roping off the prom and sands?"

"What do you think? But before I go into that, let me remind you, Bill, that you rang me last night concerning botulism and fish."

"The Birmingham do was caused by a dicey tin of salmon, and there was my missus lobbing up fish for supper. It made me think."

"Me, too."

"Hold it," said Green. "Are you saying you'd thought of the fish business before I rang you?"

"No. Your call was invaluable. It concentrated my mind."

"But you reckon you were already thinking along those lines."

"No. Don't get so het up. Let me explain and you will see what I mean. I was reading about type E. It was only then that I discovered that I had misunderstood both Convamore and Moller or, and I prefer to believe this is the more likely, that they had not briefed us fully. Bill, you are the memory man. Where did our two scientific friends say we were most likely to encounter botulism type E?"

Green frowned. "In the northern hemisphere."

"What did you take that to mean?"

"What it says."

"I'll ask the question another way. Did you take that to mean Canada, Alaska, Northern Europe, Russia . . ."

"Of course. Siberia was actually mentioned."

"You didn't include the North Atlantic, the North Pacific, the White Sea, the Baltic and every other sea north of the equator?"

"Of course I didn't," snorted Green. "Why the hell should I have done so? If somebody mentions the northern hemisphere to me, I think of the land masses, not the seas unless they are specifically mentioned."

"I made the same mistake—until I started reading those papers last night. Then I discovered that type E is predominantly found in the waters of the northern hemisphere."

"But . . ." began Green.

"Yes?"

"There was a lot of tarradiddle spoken about the scarcity of Type E in this country. Why the devil couldn't they have said that the waters round about were snived with it?"

"I think it was a case of those who know think that those who don't know actually know more than they really do."

"Go on," grunted Green, apparently too immersed in the conversation to notice the snarling traffic.

"It had occurred to me that if one is looking for the source of some disease, the most likely place to find it is where it is rife, not where it is literally so thin on the ground as to be almost imperceptible."

"Logical."

"So, in our case, we should be looking at the sea."

"Right again."

"Then you rang up and started talking about fish."

"So?"

"I was thinking about the sea, you were talking about fish. Your very convenient call—as I said—concentrated my mind."

"I follow. But all we've got are tins of contaminated ham, luncheon meat and bully beef. Not a sign of fish."

"So far."

"You reckon there'll be more cases? Ones that will involve tins of fish?"

"That's one of my fears. But if there are, we can't do anything about them."

"So what's your point, George?"

"We've been wondering how the perpetrator of this hideous business could produce pure type E botulism—if you'll forgive the term. There have been two questions to answer, actually. First, if he just used meat and vegetables, or even fish, from a fish shop and just cooked them partially, how would he get the rare type E? And having got the rare type E, how did he get it uncontaminated with salmonella and other similar nasties? I asked Moller about that one, and he couldn't give me a useful answer. But to me the answer is obvious. The type E came from the sea. Our criminal scientist did not culture his contaminant. The sea did it for him."

"Wait a moment, Chief," protested Berger. "I presume you mean the sea infected some fish."

"Right."

"But you just said that he couldn't have used fish."

"From a fish shop."

"What difference does it make whether it comes from a fish shop or not?"

"Because, laddie," said Green heavily, "botulism only attacks dead meat or fish. You were told that. If it attacked live animals, all the fish in the sea would be kaput or infected so's we couldn't eat them. The fish that finds itself on the fishmonger's slab is taken from the water while still alive and kicking. Therefore, it hasn't got botulism. Therefore, it comes in the same category as any meat and veg that Chummy might use for culturing botulism—and His Nibs has proved that that is napoo unless you want a pinch of salmonella with it. And you can't have salmonella and suchlike with it, because they would blow the tins and give the game away before it got started."

"I get all that," said Berger slowly, "but I still don't see . . ."

"Don't see what?"

"What the Chief's getting at."

"Of course you don't, lad, because it's his secret and he hasn't got there yet."

"Oh! That's a relief. I thought I was being a bit dim."

"Perish the thought, lad." Green leaned forward to address Reed. "When you can get this heap of upholstered machinery off this misbegotten racetrack, please do so. I'm in need of a large beer, and after that I'll want a drink."

"A good idea," said Masters, who always tried to please Green on car journeys. "But not a motorway pull-in. We want a decent pub, so turn off when you can."

"Right, Chief."

Green turned to him: "You were saying, George? Before young Berger gave as fine a display of ignorance as I've seen from a member of the force in years, that is?"

"I said the sea produced the botulism. You explained it had to be in dead flesh. Now apart from the carcase of a dead fish on the shore, how could you get dead fish in the sea?"

"In a can," chorused Reed and Berger together.

"Clever lads," said Green. "They're like that old comic turn—the Sisters Twizzle. Funny, isn't it, that although the Halls are a thing of the past, the old routines live on in the young?"

"Chief," said Reed breezily, "we've just heard how it is impossible for the fishmonger's fish to be contaminated with botulism, but

I could almost swear I heard of somebody who, only last night, was given Dover sole for supper and then got so worried lest it might be infected that he rang you up for reassurance."

Green had the grace to laugh. "All right. You win. And just for scoring off me, young Reed, you can buy my first pint, while young Berger can buy the drink after that."

Masters felt pleased by the atmosphere in the car. The near-hilarity, though possibly unseemly among senior detectives faced with an exceedingly serious case that was far from solved, had served to lift some of the gloom which he felt had sat heavily on them ever since they had been given the job. Each one had tried to be cheerful in his work, but until now it had been a forced, bogus cheerfulness, put on at his request. This trip—his longshot trip—seemed to have lifted their spirits. He prayed that it wouldn't be all for nothing. The let-down of a complete failure would, even among these men, hardened as they were to disaster, be difficult to take and almost impossible to reverse.

"We'll get on," he said. "After the DCI rang me to mention his fish supper, I concentrated on discovering from the papers I was reading what I could about type E and the sea. I learned a lot. First, that where types A and B are characteristically contaminants of meat and vegetables, type E attacks fish, and is particularly associated with fish.

"I also noted, in an article written about the Birmingham outbreak . . ."

"Which started with a tin of salmon," reminded Green.

"Quite. Salmon canned in Alaska."

"Which is about as far north in the northern hemisphere as you can get."

"That's quite an important point, actually," said Masters, apparently unruffled by the interruptions. "But I'll get back to that in a minute or two. For the moment, let's concentrate on the Birmingham tin of salmon.

"The scientist who wrote the paper I am telling you about stated quite categorically that type E spores are killed by heating to eighty degrees centigrade for thirty minutes. He declares that the routine canning process would have destroyed any spores present at that time because it involves heating at between a hundred and fifteen and a hundred and twenty degrees for longer than thirty minutes.

"He suggests, therefore, that though there may have been the possibility of a disruption in the factory heating routine, this is unlikely as there were no other contaminated tins."

Green grunted his approval of this obvious piece of logic, and Reed began to slow to turn off the motorway a few hundred yards ahead.

Masters continued. "The only other possibility—and this seems to be the most likely one—is that an individual can was contaminated through a minute hole after the canning was complete. I am not sure of my facts here, but I believe the cans are water-cooled . . ."

"Ah! Go on, George. This is getting interesting."

"If the organism was in the cooling water and it got through that minute hole . . . well, as the man said, one spore would have been enough—so long as no oxygen got in, too. Just one spore which subsequently grew and elaborated its toxin in the way our own boffins described to us."

Reed, who was by now coasting away from the motorway, said: "What was that about Alaskan water, Chief?"

"The DCI said that Alaska is pretty far north, implying, I suspect, that it is pretty cold up in those parts."

"Eskimo weather," agreed Green.

"Well," continued Masters, "you will be intrigued to learn that a distinctive feature of type E is that it can live, grow, and produce its toxin at four degrees centigrade, which is the temperature at which water begins to freeze and at which domestic refrigerators operate."

There was a short silence, then Green said: "Interesting, George, but why intriguing? I mean, does that particular nugget of information help us in any way?"

"At the moment, perhaps not, except to dispel the impression we were given that these organisms only spring to life when conditions are right. I most definitely imagined them lying doggo—like snakes—until the sun came to warm them up and the food was there to hand. The little bastards can do their stuff in seawater that is damn-near freezing, and I think that it was seawater which cultured the bacilli which are causing the present trouble. So, if my longshot comes off, I reckon this distinctive feature of being able to operate in the cold will be important."

"Fair enough. I'm beginning to get the drift."

"I'll leave it there for the moment, and continue after lunch," replied Masters, as Reed pulled into the forecourt of an elderly but inviting-looking inn. "What's this place?"

"The White Swan, Chief. It's not bad. If we just want a drink and a ploughman's, there's a door at the far end."

"I see it," said Green, already out of the car. "That's the place for me. The Tipsy Bar. I couldn't have thought up a better name myself. It had better come up to expectations, young Reed."

"There are a couple of nice bits of capurtle in there," replied Reed as he locked the door. "They're a great attraction, as you can see by the number of cars."

"It's the booze and food that wants to be the attraction at a pub," retorted Green, "not bits of skirt."

"Go and see for yourself. There's a cold table right down at the end. They're two student types—trained food handlers."

"Right," said Green. "I will. After all, you two lads are buying the drinks. I'll go and see what the grub's like."

"Not bad. Not bad at all," said Green as they re-entered the car forty minutes later. "I liked the one with the big bust. She had to be a bit careful, of course, when she was sharpening the carving knife—had to hold it a long way in front of her, if you get my meaning, but she was a dab hand at making sandwiches. Oh, and the beer wasn't bad either. I'm not quite sure whether that was due to good cellarage or not having to pay for it—on the principle that free beer tastes bitterest."

Berger drove this time. That left Reed, in the front passenger seat, free to turn to address Masters.

"We've heard all about botulism in the sea and how it can survive in cold water, Chief. And we've heard how you and Mrs Masters weren't allowed on the beach. Are you going to tie things up for us? Because, quite honestly, I can't see how you can link the two well enough to have us all racing down to the Isle of Wight in the middle of a big case, longshot or no longshot."

"Oh, I dunno," said Green. "It's like in Test Matches. We're having a rest-day in the middle. It's a new innovation. Something to do with counterbalancing the unsocial hours that coppers have to work."

"You seem happy about it, anyway."

"Course I am, lad."

"You reckon the Chief's guess will come off?"

"I didn't say that. But he has been known to be right before, and as there's nothing else we can do in this case except play guessing games, I've no option but to go along with him, and like it."

"Gracious," murmured Masters.

Green helped himself to a Kensitas from a crumpled packet, ignoring Reed's obvious expectation of being offered a cigarette. As he lit up, he glanced across at Masters. "Well," he said, "are you going to tell us, or not?"

Masters waited just a moment before he began. Then—

"I told you that Wanda and I were ordered off the beach by a constable. Whilst I was having a word or two to say about his manners, his sergeant arrived."

"And proceeded to get it in the neck, too, I suppose."

"No. He had information."

"Ah! Lucky chap."

"He reminded me of something I think we were all aware of at the time it happened late last year."

"It?"

"Bad weather that sank several small freighters . . ."

"Got it," grinned Green, his memory clicking into top gear. A Greek job called the *Aeolian Sky*, last November, sometime, off Dorset."

"Among others," admitted Masters admiringly. "Several of them lost deck cargo and so, as you can imagine, a hell of a lot of material went into the sea in that general area. And among the jetsam there would have been food—tinned food—crates of it, for feeding the crew of those freighters, in addition to any cargoes of food they may have been carrying."

"Tinned food," said Green softly. "Hundreds and hundreds of tins of 'herrings in' and pink salmon." He turned to Masters. "I think I can guess the rest of the story. The *Aeolian Sky* was carrying canisters of poison, wasn't she?"

"That's right. She went down in November, and while I was in the Isle of Wight in the spring with Wanda, there were reports of dead whales being washed up on the south coast and then—when the wind and tide were right for it—the canisters began to be washed up on the Isle of Wight beaches."

"The sergeant told you this by way of explanation for his constable kicking you off the beach?"

"Yes. But he went further. He'd got the names of the poisons written down. They were arsenic trichloride, amino methyl propanol and phenyl benzanine."

"I don't blame him for writing that lot down," said Reed. "They're a bit of a mouthful. Are they as nasty as they sound, Chief?"

"As I understand it, they are chemicals used in manufacturing processes but are, nevertheless, highly dangerous. The Isle of Wight authorities reclaimed over nine hundred canisters of various sizes."

"Canned food and canned poison," said Green, "all being washed up together."

"That is my point," said Masters. "Firemen were employed to collect the poison canisters, but I learned that there were so many of them, of different shapes, sizes and sorts, that the authorities felt it safer to call in all the chemists and scientists they could lay their hands on to identify the poison canisters for the firemen to collect."

"I remember something of that," said Green. "Didn't I read that they'd rounded up the chemistry masters from the schools to help?"

"Quite right."

Green nodded. "But we can forget the poisons, can't we? Our only interest in them is that they attracted a number of scientists to beaches where tins of fish were being washed up."

"That is my longshot."

"And a very good one, too. Whether it comes off or not, it had to be tried," said Green handsomely. "A scientist picking up a tin of salmon off the beach and putting it in his pocket for . . ." He turned to Masters. "For what, George? How would he know it was impregnated with botulism?"

Masters shrugged. "I honestly can't give you an answer to that, Bill. I don't know whether he was aware of the facts of the Birmingham case and examined for a hole in the tin. I don't know whether he had his plan in mind before he discovered the tin, or whether the tin put the idea into his head. As I have stressed repeatedly, this is a longshot. But I do know one thing that could be—or rather, might be—of interest."

"What's that?"

"The Ministry of Agriculture and Fisheries has a laboratory at Burnham-on-Crouch, and the scientists there were involved in tests on those dead whales that were washed up—to determine whether they had been killed by the *Aeolian Sky*'s chemicals or not."

Green shook his head. "You're not suggesting that government boffins would be so stupid and criminal as to spread botulism, are you, George?"

"The answer to that is no, I think not and I hope not. But when I was thinking this through last night, I was aware that we had agreed that our man would need a laboratory in which to operate. It was, if you like to regard it as such, one of the obstacles to my idea. And it was my job to try to demolish as many obstacles as possible so that I could determine whether or not this trip was not only feasible, but justifiable. So, when I remembered that the Min. of Ag. and Fish had been involved with the whales, I looked up to find out where they operated from. I was expecting a list of little offices all round the coast, but there, large as life, was the address of their laboratory in Burnham. I do not suggest they are likely to interest us in any way professionally, but you must admit it was a chance to get rid of one obstacle in my mind that I'd have been a fool to overlook."

"I know what you mean," grunted Green. "And if it's any comfort to you, I'd have done exactly the same."

"In case you hadn't noticed," cut in Berger, "we are now approaching the ferry terminal."

"And about time, too," said Green, certainly not deploring the lack of speed, but thankful to be out of the hated car.

Chapter 6

GREEN WAS THOUGHTFUL on the boat journey to the island. He stood on deck silent for some time, allowing the breeze to ruffle his hair and clothing, as though wrestling with some mental problem. Eventually he joined Masters who was sitting on a slatted seat on the lee side, smoking and watching the movement of the water as the tub-like vessel nudged its way towards Cowes.

"George."

"Yes, Bill?" Masters moved to make room for Green.

"We'll be working on the Chief Constable of Hampshire's patch. Is he going to like it?"

"As to that, I can't say, Bill."

"You didn't phone him to say we were coming?"

"No. But I'm not disregarding the courtesies. Bob Wigglesworth has sent a Home Office circular letter to all authorities."

"Saying what?"

"Basically to warn them that there is a widespread botulism outbreak which could reach their patches and to be on the look-out and to liaise with Health Authorities if their drills for coping with such emergencies are a little rusty."

"Does it mention us?"

"Anderson saw it and says it leaves us free to operate where we like. It apparently says that you and I are co-ordinating the enquiries . . ."

"Into the criminal background?"

"Lest there should be criminal activity is how it has been worded. All authorities have been required to offer us full co-operation at any time during the investigation, which is of a national character, etcetera, etcetera."

"So nobody will mind us just dropping in?"

"In theory, no. In practice . . ." He shrugged. "We'll try to oil the wheels, Bill, and not to be too imperious."

"Good. But it has occurred to me that since you'd had one brush with these people . . ."

"Of a very minor nature."

"But duly reported by PC Plod and his sergeant in case of repercussions."

"I suppose so."

"And if, on top of that, this longshot of yours should fail . . ."

Masters looked at him and grinned. "Bill, I believe you are anxious that I should not make myself look a proper Charlie—as indeed I would if, after being angry with some of their people, I then fell down on the job. Is that it?"

"Something of the sort."

"What are you suggesting? That I play this low-key?"

Green nodded.

"Are you really frightened I'm making a nonsense of this?"

"Not frightened you're making a nonsense of it. I'm just frightened of the case itself. We've never had one like this before—as important as this, I mean, where we're faced with tracking down a multi-murderer who may be killing people as we sit here. I said it was a bastard right from the beginning, and everybody else—you, Anderson, Doris, Wanda, everybody—says there's need for speed. As if we didn't know."

"What's your point, Bill?"

"There isn't any case, George. Nothing to get to grips with. Even you recognise this. You must do, otherwise you wouldn't have been rabbiting on about longshots as you have been doing all day, and although you often play hunches, not even you would have contemplated playing this one if there'd have been one single, solid fact to work on back home." He held up his hand to stop Masters from interrupting. "I know you've made out a reasonable cause—not a case—for coming down here, but you as good as admitted that you had to disregard the obstacles or demolish them with bits of self-deception like thinking that the Min. of Ag. and Fish laboratory can be regarded as a possible centre for transferring the organisms. And look at us—all of us—behaving like kids on a school treat to fool ourselves we're doing a good job or nearing completion. More self-deception, George."

"I agree with a lot of what you've said, Bill, but I don't believe we are deceiving ourselves. We all know the state of play."

"It must be me getting old, then."

"And it's not that either, Bill. I want to thank you for advising me to keep a low profile on the Island. I've been thinking it over, and I reckon you're right. If any one of the coppers we're going to visit thinks we're looking for a tin or a canister which was taken from their beaches—and which they were supposed to prevent being taken away—they are going to be non-co-operative. They're not going to like the idea of us laying the blame for this botulism outbreak on their carelessness and so they are going to be conveniently forgetful—convenient for them, that is—and this trip of ours is going to be abortive even though it may otherwise be exactly the right answer."

Green selected a bent Kensitas.

"So what's your plan, George?"

"With your agreement, we won't mention tins and canisters or the possibility of any of them having been smuggled off the beach. We will stick to personalities."

"The fact that we've come here at all will set them thinking."

"Let them think. I don't suppose it will harm them. And, of course, we could be misjudging them, but we'll give them no room to wriggle."

Green nodded.

"You're still not very cheerful, Bill."

Green flicked his half-smoked cigarette over the rail and watched it float down into the sea there to be extinguished only a second or so before a gull swept down on it. He looked round at Masters and said: "For a clever bloke, you're a bit of a fool at times, George."

"What do I answer to that?"

"Nothing. But you might just ask yourself why a normally cheerful bloke like me . . ."

"Go on."

"Feels ghastly on board ship."

Masters stared for a moment, and then said: "I'm very sorry, Bill. I didn't realise you were a poor sailor. We're almost there, and the sickness disappears once you set foot on dry land, doesn't it?"

Green grinned weakly. "I once travelled to Ryde with Wanda."

"So you did. She never told me . . ."

"She didn't know. Any more than you did until I told you. Besides, she was better company."

"Oh, yes? And I suspect there was a flat calm?"

"I would like a word with Sergeant Gardam if that is possible. Or failing him, Constable Crowther, please."

The desk sergeant stood with his hands wide apart on the counter top which separated him from Masters. He appeared not to have noticed Green, Reed and Berger who hovered in the background.

"Oh yes, sir? May I know the nature of your enquiry?"

"Certainly. I met them when I was here on the island in the spring and I'd now like a word with one or the other of them."

"Personal call, it is, sir? If so I must tell you we don't encourage . . ."

"Strictly business," replied Masters.

The desk sergeant pulled the incident book towards him. "In that case, sir, if you'd please tell me . . ." He took the cap off a ballpoint. "What was it you wanted?"

"To know the name of their Inspector."

The sergeant looked up, suspicion in his eyes. "And why would you want to know that, sir?"

"It's not an official secret, is it?"

"No, sir. But if you've come to make a complaint . . ."

"Nothing was further from my thoughts."

The sergeant took up his pen and started writing. "Name?"

"Masters."

"Address?"

"New Scotland Yard."

"New Scot . . ." The sergeant looked up. "Now see here, sir, if this is some sort of game . . ."

"I assure you it isn't, Sergeant. Here is my warrant card."

The sergeant looked at it. "If you'd said so in the beginning, sir . . ."

"Why should I have done so? I didn't want to make a complaint or report an incident. All I asked was to have a word with Gardam or Crowther, both of whom I met some months ago."

"You said official business, sir."

"To enquire the name of a superior officer."

The sergeant didn't reply. He closed the book.

"I can tell you his name, sir."

"Thank you."

"Inspector Jasper."

"Thank you. Would you mind asking him if my three colleagues and I could have a few words with him?"

The desk sergeant seemed to wake up to the fact that there was a team of four present. "There's nothing wrong is there, sir? I mean . . ."

"Sergeant, there is so little wrong that had you told me where I could have found Gardam or Crowther, none of this would have happened. Please tell Inspector Jasper we are here."

The sergeant lifted the phone, and inside a minute a uniformed inspector had appeared, ready to escort them to his office.

"You know, lad," said Green to Jasper, "your crowd are too neutral."

"How do you mean?"

"They're not active in doing good. They don't do any harm, but they don't seem positive in trying to help. That desk sergeant of yours, for instance, was not obstructive exactly, but neither was he co-operative until the Chief Superintendent shoved a warrant card under his nose." Green drew a chair up with his foot and sat heavily. "What I'm saying is that he invited the pulling of rank and then got nervous in case something was wrong."

Jasper carried a chair across to Masters. "I'm sorry about that, sir."

"Don't be. The DCI is merely giving you a bit of advice, much as I sent you a suggestion earlier in the year via Sergeant Gardam."

Jasper rubbed one ear. "I remember, sir. About warning the

public about those nine hundred canisters of poison that we salvaged. Was that what you wished to see me about?"

"First off," said Masters. "Have you been told of the botulism outbreak on the mainland?"

"An official warning came in yesterday."

"Did it mention that we were co-ordinating the investigation into its cause?"

"It said a team from the Yard, sir. No names were given."

"Fair enough. But you were, I believe, instructed to give us any help we might ask for."

"Yes, sir."

"Good. Now then, Mr Jasper, we can go back to the time when you were fishing poison canisters out of the sea."

"Wait a minute, sir. What's that got to do with a botulism outbreak on the mainland?"

"Laddie," said Green. "It's a long, long story, which we haven't got time to tell, or you to listen to. But we reckon there's a likelihood you can help us."

"The two are connected, then?"

"We think so," said Masters. "Or should I say there is a possibility that they are."

Jasper looked bemused. Nobody appreciated more than Masters the almost impossible mental task of linking the salvage of poison canisters with botulism, without the details that went between. His problem was how much to tell the local man. Green had scented danger in saying much about the canisters themselves. It had been agreed that they would stick, as far as possible, to personalities. Masters decided to stick to the agreement.

"Mr Jasper, we are looking for a scientist. We neither know his name nor his particular speciality, but we have reason to believe he was on the island at the time of the spring storms when the canisters were washed up."

"Are you suggesting he pinched one of those canisters, sir? Because if you are, I can tell you he didn't. We took damn good care none of them was carted off."

Green came in. "Look, lad, if we thought you'd let a gallon of poison slip through your hands, we'd have said so. We're not interested in your tin cans. It's a man we're after—perhaps a woman, but we think not—anyway, a scientist of some sort. Now think. We have good reason to believe he was on your patch right at the time when you rounded up everybody with scientific knowledge that you could get hold of to identify and handle that poison. There's a possibility, therefore, that our chap was on your list of helpers. If we can have that list it could perhaps narrow our search."

"I see. What's this scientist done?"

"That, lad, remains to be seen."

"You think he caused this botulism?"

"There's a chance that he did," said Masters. "So you'll appreciate how important it is that we have your list and—equally important—that we interview everybody involved as quickly as possible."

Jasper shook his head. "We didn't keep a list."

"No?" demanded Green heavily.

"No, sir. Look at it this way. If we are looking for a lost child, say, we get scads of people turning out to help with the search. But we don't take lists of names. We just get on with the job."

"But these were specialists, for a special job."

"I know that, sir, but it was an emergency. We've got quite a few scientists of various sorts on the island. There's quite a lot of industry—light industry that uses a lot of research people more than shop-floor workers. There's plastics, aircraft building, boat building, and all sorts of perfume, hygiene products and so on that are tested, researched and bottled here. We just sent out a call for all specialist personnel that could be spared. We even got science masters from schools."

"Who decided that you had got scientific specialists and not just any old Tom, Dick and Harry who thought he would muscle in?" asked Masters.

Jasper shrugged.

"Nobody?"

"They vouched for each other. Every one of them was known to somebody else. In an island this size, divided up into pockets of population, they all know somebody who knows somebody who

126

knows somebody. It's as simple as that."

"I understand perfectly," said Masters amiably. "I'm a great believer in such local community spirit and knowledge myself. Unfortunately, it doesn't help us much at this juncture. So, we'll have to reconstruct your non-existent list."

"Anything I can do to help, sir," said Jasper dejectedly. "You've only to ask."

"Despite what you said about a lot of research-based industry here, there couldn't have been many scientists involved."

"Twenty or so. Less than thirty, definitely."

Masters turned to Green. "We ought to be able to winkle out that number easily enough."

"Given a start by our friend here—a few names."

Jasper seemed eager to recover lost ground. "I'll see to that straight away. You could have the first of them quite quickly. The fire service took care of the canisters. I'm sure they'll be able to help, too."

"Thank you." Masters glanced at his watch. "It is getting on for six o'clock now. See what you can do for us overnight, Mr Jasper. We'll be here bright and early in the morning. Perhaps you would lend us a couple of guides for the day—uniformed men, so that not too many questions are asked about our presence here. I don't want to upset the even tenor of holiday life, and plain clothes men are not as readily accepted without question."

"Two sergeants, sir?"

"Why not those two the Chief Super met in the spring?" asked Green. "Gardam and Crowther. I'm sure they'd like to renew the acquaintance."

Jasper laughed. "I'm not so sure about that—from the way Sergeant Gardam told the story. Still, if that's what Mr Masters wants . . ."

"That would suit me very well," said Masters. "It will give all three of us a chance to bury the hatchet."

"The trouble is," said Green, as they stood in the bar of their hotel in Ryde, "that even you, George, have become pessimistic about this one."

"Have you, Chief?" asked Reed.

Masters grimaced. "Pessimistic? Perhaps. But I think the real trouble is I won't allow myself to relax."

"I don't get it."

"This is a very serious case. One which, itself, has given us no help."

"I like that thought," said Green, taking the last Kensitas from the packet. "Always before, the field has been limited. Big sometimes. Perhaps a thousand or so suspects to begin with. That means that at least you have an area to concentrate your work in. But, always, when there isn't a limited field and you get no sort of a hint from a grass, a case becomes a headache. Take just one example. That Yorkshire Ripper business. An unlimited field to begin with. Then the local boys narrowed it down to somebody from the north of England, then the North East and finally—due to the fact that the bloke recorded his own voice and sent it to the police—they have been able to name the town, almost the street where he was born and brought up. But there's just something missing. His Nibs said the case itself had given no help. Somebody else might say they haven't had the necessary bit of luck. But it's more than that. Luck suggests something quick—like a coincidence or a chance remark overheard—whereas help from the case itself would come perhaps from all the months and years of routine work those lads have put in. Nothing has come up."

"You're saying this case is like that?"

"Exactly. Just as they narrowed the field to an area in the North East, we've narrowed the field to a scientist or a scientific technician. Well, there must be scores of thousands of them about. We're doing the routine stuff, too. That's why we're looking into people who might think they have been done down by Redcokes. But how long will that take to bear fruit, if it ever does?"

"Never, most likely," said Berger. "Grudges like that are usually secret ones. What I mean is, if people sound off about what they'd like to do to people who've done them dirt, they never actually do it. They let off steam by shouting about it. But secret grudges, they fester away in silence until they blow up like a volcano erupting and cause the owners to take drastic action. And the owners may well be mild-mannered people who have become embittered."

"Right, lad," agreed Green. "So when His Nibs says the case isn't helping us, he's right. And we're reduced to guessing—at least, he is."

"But," said Reed, "this guess of the Chief's has all the hallmarks of . . ."

"Of what, lad?"

"Well, it makes sense to me."

"You mean it *could* make sense," said Masters. "That's my point. A guess is a quickie, like the bits of luck or chance remarks the DCI mentioned earlier. And the essence of a quickie is that one should put it to the test immediately. While the enthusiasm for it is still red hot."

"What you're saying, Chief, is that not having been able to test your theory today has taken the steam out of it?"

"To some degree. I've been given time to realise just how monstrously coincidental it would be if the guess paid off. It means I'm a lot less sanguine than I was last night when I first thought of it."

"If you'll allow me to say so, Chief, you're looking at this from the wrong point of view."

"Am I?" asked Masters, surprised by the sergeant's tone as well as his words. "What makes you think so?"

"You've all along said this jaunt was a longshot. So it is. But a longshot is not just a guess. At least, this one isn't. You've worked it out by deduction based on knowledge. That's not just a guess. It's the way all egg-head academics discover things and push out the boundaries of knowledge. I know what you're feeling. You reckon there are so many other things you ought to be doing. Interviewing those botulism patients, perhaps. But there's nothing else you can do. Those patients can't talk. Their throats are paralysed. You've been stopped from warning the public. You'd be no good helping Convamore and Moller in their laboratories. You wouldn't be as good as local police in searching out local grievances. You've started everything up and now all you can do is sit back and wait—or try longshots like this. It may not pay off, but

129

that doesn't mean it's not worth trying. At any rate, I believe in it."

"Thank you."

"Well said, lad," said Green. "Just for that I'll buy the next round."

"It's time for dinner."

"Is it? Good. That lets me out."

"You could always buy a bottle of vino for the table."

"Vino? Be your age, young Reed. I'd want white and you'd want red, and before I knew where I was I'd have paid enough corkage to buy the pub itself."

"You don't pay corkage on bottles you buy here."

"Inflated prices, then. Same thing. I have a strong belief that no bottle of table wine is worth more than five bob. That's my top limit."

As they entered the diningroom, Green stopped for a word with the head waiter. A moment or two later a litre bottle of medium dry Monte Cristo Montilla appeared on the table. "Now this," said Green, picking it up, "is better and cheaper than plonk. Try it. It goes with anything."

"You've been here before."

"Many times."

"Why?" asked Masters. "Bearing everything in mind."

Green looked across at him. "Doris likes it."

Masters nodded his understanding.

Jasper said: "I think we've got nearly all of them for you."

"Excellent." Masters sounded in high spirits. It was a gorgeous morning, so much so that even Green had enjoyed the car journey from Ryde. In addition, Masters had salved his conscience by ringing his office and speaking to Lake who reassured him that nothing of any moment had happened in his absence. Now that the chance to prove whether his longshot was on target or wide of the mark had arrived he had cheered considerably. This, in turn, had cheered Green who believed matters always looked rosier in the evening than in the harsh light of a new day. If Masters had reversed this belief then it was for him, Green, a good sign: almost an augury of success.

"Fourteen names," said Jasper. "Of course, I couldn't contact everybody, and people tend to forget, but if you question those you have there, sir, you should get a few more."

"Thank you. And our guides?"

"In the car park. Crowther has a Panda car. I expected you would want to borrow it, seeing that you only have the one vehicle with you."

"That was very thoughtful of you. I was going to ask if you could let us have a car."

"Anything I can do for you, sir, I will. On one condition."

"What's that?"

"That you let me know what is really happening—when it's all over, that is."

"The pleasure will be ours, lad," said Green. "Now, let's have that list . . ."

After Masters had found and introduced Sergeant Gardam and a very sheepish Constable Crowther, he said to them all: "We have here fourteen names. My first thought on getting this list was that those who figure on it are obviously fairly well-known men for one reason or another. That suggests that they live here permanently and, though they may go to and from the mainland occasionally, I shouldn't imagine that they are the sort who get about there quite as much as our man obviously did—from Somerset, to Derby, to Colchester, to Bournemouth and heaven knows where else."

"You mean the list is no good, Chief."

"No, I don't mean that. But I suspect that the names on it will not contain the one we want, and . . ." he turned to Gardam, ". . . is there a Redcoke store or supermarket anywhere on the island, Sergeant?"

"No, sir. You know the policy here? None of the big chain stores is allowed to open up in case they put the locals out of business."

"Thank you. I thought that was so." He continued to address the rest of them. "So you see it is unlikely that anybody who actually lives here or has lived here for any great length of time will have been subjected to a raw deal from the Redcokes property division."

"What do we do about it, Chief?"

"We interview each of these people in turn and during the course of the interviews we ask them for the names of any scientist who worked with them. In that way we should expand the list until, eventually, we really have met everybody concerned. So please keep the lists carefully and get to know whereabouts each person was working."

"We might be able to compile a map," said Green. "You never know, it might tell us something."

"True. Perhaps you can tell us, Sergeant Gardam, how many days the search took."

"Three days, sir. Not that there was much to be found on the third day, though we had one or two calls of sightings up to a week later."

"I see. Get the days each scientist worked, too. Then the DCI can cover each day. My wife and I left the island on the Wednesday, so the first day of the search would be Tuesday."

"Joe," said Green, addressing Constable Crowther. "You were down on the beach that first day . . ."

"All three days, sir."

"Better still. Besides those poison canisters, was there a lot of other stuff thrown up on the beach?"

"You name it, sir, and it was there. We got cartloads of timber, bits of clothing, even an old alarm clock and a few grapefruit."

"Tins of food?"

"Quite a few, sir, but we were careful about them. They've most of 'em got their labels soaked off and they'd been close to those cans of poison. They were collected and dumped."

"You mean nothing was taken from the beaches?"

"I'm not saying that, sir, because all the wood was, and I know for a fact that a life belt and a couple of jackets disappeared from a heap. So it's likely other stuff went as well."

"We concentrated on seeing nothing dangerous went missing, Mr Green," said Gardam. "The poison was kept strictly separate under guard the whole time."

"Fair enough," said Green airily enough to give the two local men the impression that a few things wandering off was of no consequence. "Now, George, if I could have seven of those names . . ."

Masters handed the list over and told off Crowther to drive Green and Berger, while Gardam was to accompany himself and Reed. "Report in here, by phone, please. After every interview. We can keep in touch with each other that way if needs be."

It was a wearying task on so hot a day. The same questions over and over again; the jogging of reluctant memories—reluctant because long days on cold wind-swept beaches are best forgotten; who were your companions? were there any whom you didn't know personally or didn't know by repute? which beaches did you scour? did you remove anything from them? do you know anybody who did remove anything? After that, questions as to whether the one being interviewed had a laboratory at his disposal or did he work with slide rule and calculator. A quick inspection of the working area of the few who had access to laboratories.

Then, because it was high summer, some were on holiday. Were they away or were they spending their leave at home?

Masters decided to have lunch at the little pub in Cowes which he and Wanda had visited. It was overcrowded. They had to queue up and choose their food and be given a numbered ticket before pressing into the bar for a drink. It did little to refresh them after so hot and abortive a morning. Fortunately, Gardam's uniform won him instant attention at the bar, and the wait for cold beer was not a long one.

"We're not getting anywhere, Chief."

Masters, determined not to give way to further pessimism, replied: "I think we are. This exercise was bound to appear abortive unless we were lucky enough to strike oil very early on. Besides, we are eliminating them one by one. Virtually none of them has been to the mainland since Easter, for example."

"We haven't tested their claims, Chief."

"Not at the moment. We may have to, of course."

"If we do, and find a discrepancy . . ."

"It could help, or merely mean that the boffin in question is forgetful."

Gardam brought the beer.

"You're having a fairly thin time, Sergeant, just acting as guide."

"Don't worry about me, sir. It's as good a day as any to wait about doing nothing or riding round the island in your Rover."

"You've done the ringing in after each interview," reminded Reed.

Gardam grinned. "Hard work that is. I don't think I'll manage to endure the cracks I'm getting from Dave Wright—the desk sergeant. Which reminds me, sir, I'd better get out to a phone for this last call. It's nearly two o'clock."

"Is it that time already?"

"Watch my beer," said Gardam to Reed.

"Finish it first," said Masters. "We'll look after your sandwiches when they come."

Gardam swallowed the last of his beer and pushed his way out of the bar. "Get him—and us—another," said Masters to Reed. "You just might have them by the time he gets back."

In the event, both beer and sandwiches were on the little corner table Masters had managed to secure by the time Gardam returned. He looked hot and excited.

"Sorry to have been so long, sir, but there was somebody using the kiosk, and I didn't want to speak from here with this crowd listening."

"Sit down and have your lunch."

"No time for that, sir, I'm afraid. DCI Green wants to see you. He's in a pub in Yarmouth."

"Sit down," ordered Masters. "Have your sandwiches and tell me exactly what the message was."

Gardam spoke with his mouth full.

"Sergeant Wright said Mr Green rang in, at about twenty to two. What he said was to tell you when you next rang in that he was just going to have lunch at the pub in Yarmouth, and if you wanted to enjoy a bite, you'd join him there as soon as you could."

"He said a bite?"

"Yes, sir."

"Good enough, Chief," said Reed. "He means he's got a nibble, and a good one, but he wouldn't say so straight out—knowing him."

Masters felt the excitement and the relief growing within him, but he strove to keep his voice matter-of-fact.

"We'll finish our lunch here in peace. No rushing. The DCI likes a good lunch break and whatever he has won't spoil. Take your time, Gardam. Don't give yourself indigestion."

Despite Masters' exhortations, the two sergeants were ready to travel inside five minutes.

"We'll have to go back nearly into Newport and then turn right," instructed Gardam. Masters settled back in the car, took off his jacket, loosened his tie, lowered the car window and began to pack his pipe. "Take it easy, Reed. We want to get there in one piece."

In the tiny town of Yarmouth, in a side road which ran between the approach to the pier and the harbour, Reed pulled up the Rover behind Crowther's Panda car. Through the open sash window of the pub, Masters saw Green sprawling on a bench seat with half a tankard of beer still in front of him. Green looked out as Masters got down.

"Don't bother to come in, George. They've called time in here. They're wanting us out."

"Sit in the shade, you lot," ordered Green to the four sergeants. "I want a word in private with His Nibs." He then led the way out of the little side street and crossed over to the rails around the harbour. They managed to find a few spare feet not occupied by the sightseers who were watching the activity on the fleet of motor cruisers in the basin.

"Not bad," muttered Green, nodding towards one craft on top of the cabin of which was lying a girl with a skin the colour of teak, set off by a yellow bikini.

"Not bad at all," agreed Masters, determined not to ask Green why he had been summoned.

Green helped himself to a cigarette.

"Nice place this. Doris and I often come here or else round the other side where they've provided seats on a pretty bit of green that runs down to the water."

"Wanda and I went there. Doris told her about it."

"Did you get to Alum Bay?"

"Not up and down all the steps. Wanda wouldn't have managed them."

"I suppose not."

There was a silence for a few moments after this exchange, then Green said, laconically, "I may have found him, George."

"Thanks, Bill."

"I only said may."

"I heard. But you've got a nose."

"I suppose so. Want to know how far I've got?"

"Please."

"There's a young industrial chemist here called Chapman. He works in one of those buildings on that new estate behind us across the road. He told me what he does, but I don't understand half of it. Something to do with control testing of something they make over there. He goes and takes odd samples and puts them under a microscope to see they're up to standard or dissolves them in water to see how long they take to disappear."

"I know the rudiments of testing."

"I thought you would."

"Is that all?"

"All I'm going to tell you. Chapman himself can tell you the rest. He's expecting us."

Green turned from the railing and with Masters alongside him, crossed the road close to the bus stop and turned into the new industrial estate nearby. Green opened the door of the third single-storied building.

"Mr Chapman's expecting me again, love."

The girl spoke into the internal phone and then looked up at Green. "You know your way, don't you?"

"Ta, love."

It was a small office with the storm vents wide open to let in a little air and a lot of noise. Chapman, Masters guessed, was about twenty-seven or eight. A good-looking young man, big-built and fair as a Viking.

"Mr Ronald Chapman," announced Green. "Detective Chief Superintendent Masters."

136

Chapman shook hands and said: "You're a bit overwhelming, you two," and laughed a little nervously. "Sit down, please."

"Now, Ronnie lad," began Green. "I want you to tell my boss exactly what you told me and answer any questions he has." He turned to Masters. "Ron was anxious to get home to lunch, so I didn't hold him up once I'd established that he had something to tell us. He's not long been married, you see, and he goes home for lunch and his little missus gets worried if he's a bit late."

Chapman reddened, as if suspecting that Green was laughing at him. He was relieved to hear Masters say: "If I could get home to my wife at lunchtime, I'd be there. I've got a baby son, too, Mr Chapman. I don't see as much of him as I'd like on full working days."

"Yes, well . . ." Chapman cleared his throat. "Mr Green came to ask me if I'd helped with picking up the poison canisters. The point is, I did and I didn't." He paused as if expecting some comment, but getting none, continued. "The police asked the firm if they would give me time off to help. My boss agreed, but it was inconvenient for me. The call came from my boss while I was having breakfast in my digs . . ."

"On the Tuesday morning?" asked Masters.

"That's right. He told me to report direct to the fire chief at the beach, dressed in old clothes and rubber boots. But the point was, you see, I was getting married next day, Wednesday. I'd got everything arranged. I was coming in here till lunchtime to get things straight for my holiday, then I was taking the afternoon off to get a haircut and do a bit of shopping. I had to buy the bridesmaids a little gift each, and one for my best man. You know the form . . ."

"We've all experienced it," agreed Masters.

"So you can see that when I got that phone call that morning I wasn't too happy."

"Returned to the breakfast table swearing a bit, did you, lad?"

"Wouldn't you?"

Green inclined his head.

"Well, my digs were in a boarding house—Mrs Dutton's in Newport. I was the only full-time lodger she had then. They like full-timers in the winter, you know, but not in the summer, because they can charge holiday makers more than regulars. That's why Sue and I were getting married before the holiday rush started."

Masters nodded and waited for Chapman to carry on, letting him tell his story in his own way.

"Anyhow, there was one other chap at Mrs Dutton's—on holiday by himself. A thin, nervous sort of chap, about thirty, I'd say, and he was sitting opposite me at breakfast. He asked me what was wrong, so I told him. Then he said that I needn't worry, he would stand in for me as he'd nothing to do much except go down to the beach, so he might as well make himself useful."

"But . . ." protested Masters, "you had been called in as a chemist. How could this man take your place?"

"Because he was a scientist, too. Not a chemist. A cryophysicist actually. We'd talked about it the night before over supper, so I knew he was genuine."

"And that," said Green, "is where I stopped Ron. As soon as I heard the word cryophysicist, I knew this was going to be up your alley, George, not mine. So I let Ron go off for lunch and phoned for you."

"Thanks, Bill." Masters turned to Chapman. "What was this man's name?"

"Wilkin. Stephen Wilkin."

"Please go on with your story."

"That's it, really. I took Wilkin down and said I'd come from the firm. The fire chief was too busy really to pay much attention to what I said about only helping him for the morning. He just said every little helps and accepted Wilkin on my say-so. Happy to get him, I suppose."

"And that is all you know?"

"Absolutely. We were sent off in different directions and I packed it in at one o'clock. I didn't see Wilkin again, because I had a stag party that night and I wasn't back at the digs until all hours. Next day, Wilkin was up and gone before I was ready to move—I had to pack the last of my things, you see, because I wasn't going back to Mrs Dutton's after the wedding. We'd bought one of the new houses here in Yarmouth, and I was dumping my kit here."

"Quite. You've been very helpful, Mr Chapman."

"I have?"

"Most certainly. Can you please tell me where Mr Wilkin lived and worked?"

"Sorry. We never got round to details like that. But I expect Ma Dutton will have his address."

"Of course."

"By the way, Chief Superintendent."

"Yes?"

"You haven't told me what all this is about, and why you're looking for Wilkin. Do you think he pinched a canister of arsenic trichloride or something?"

"We have no reason to believe that any of the poison canisters went missing, Mr Chapman."

"I should think not. Those chemicals were killing mammals as big as whales, and nobody but a fool would fiddle with them. And Wilkin wasn't a fool."

"No?"

"He was a bright boy. Rather intense, you know. Earnest, I suppose you'd call him. One of the sort that has the cares of the world on his shoulders."

"What had he to say about canisters of chemicals finding their way into the sea?"

"He got very het up about the dumping of chemical waste and their indiscriminate use. Big business seemed to be one of his bugbears—big business that wasn't sponsoring research that is."

"What sort of research?"

"His own, of course. What else?" Chapman laughed. "It's funny how even scientists who are taught to take a logical, dispassionate point of view can always see the blue eyes of their own particular babies."

"You said he was a cryophysicist. Now I'm aware that the suffix cryo has to do with low temperatures, but I thought that cryogenics was the branch of physics concerned with phenomena at very low temperatures."

"Same thing, virtually," said Chapman. "Not that it's something I know very much about."

"I know nothing about it," grunted Green. "Give me a bit of a run-down, Ron, just so's I'm not entirely in the dark. What do you say, George?"

"I'd like to hear what Mr Chapman can tell us, as long as he makes it intelligible to the lay mind."

"Well now," said Chapman, "Let's see how best to put it. I suppose I can say it is the science dealing with the production of very low temperatures and the study of their physical and technological consequences."

"By very low," asked Masters, "are we talking about hundreds of degrees below zero?"

"At a guess, I'd say everything below minus a hundred and fifty centigrade or Celsius, if you prefer it."

"How's that?" asked Green.

"Celsius was the scientist who standardised what we call the centigrade scale. Both scales put the melting point of ice at nought and the boiling point of water at a hundred. However, that's by the way. What a layman should latch on to is that at very low temperatures indeed, matter develops some very remarkable properties."

"Like what?"

"I really don't know a lot about it—I don't think that anybody is completely clued up on it because all the study of the cryo world is essentially a recent science. It really started when people discovered how to liquefy gases—including helium which, as I understand it, proved the toughest."

"Like they liquefy natural gas in Canada to transport it in tankers?"

"Right. Liquid gas takes up only a tiny, tiny part of the volume occupied by its gaseous equivalent. That's one of the results of cryophysics. It makes it easy to transport natural gas as they would oil."

"What other special phenomena are there connected with cryophysics?"

"I suspect there are thousands. But you must know about superconductivity, for instance."

"Never heard of it," said Green.

"Well, many metals and alloys show the property of

superconductivity at very low temperatures. What happens is that the metal assumes a state in which its electrical resistance has entirely vanished. That means that electric currents can flow through it indefinitely without generating heat or losing their own strength. So you can see that if you need, for instance, a very strong magnetic field, you just keep coils of wire very cold by using liquid helium and push electricity through them. They don't need anything like the amount of current ordinary electromagnets need and, what is more, their fields remain very constant."

"Interesting," murmured Masters. "Any other applications that you know of?"

"Liquefied gases for rocket propulsion, magnets and . . . yes, tissue freezing techniques have been used in surgery."

"Ah! Anything concerning food?"

"I'm sure there must be. The possibilities are endless, but I don't know of any specifically to do with food, though if you can freeze human tissue for surgery I can see no reason why animal flesh cannot be treated with some advantage."

"Quite. One last question about cryophysicists. Would a man engaged in them need to be a fairly expert technician?"

"I honestly don't know, but my guess would be yes. You'll gather from what I've told you that so far, at any rate, all the applications are intensely practical. It's fair to say that practical applications have to be researched in labs—on a small scale, of course—before even a viable pilot scheme can be built outside."

"Thank you." Masters got to his feet. "That really was the last question on that particular subject, Mr Chapman, and we're in your debt."

"I've helped?"

"Tremendously."

"I noticed that you sidestepped very neatly when I asked you exactly what you are investigating."

"It's difficult to tell you, Ron," said Green. "Chiefly because we don't want to be unfair to your pal Wilkin if we are on the wrong track. But we can safely say that we are on the biggest case we two have ever been on—or any other coppers for that matter. So keep it to yourself, chum."

"Of course. Thank you for telling me."

"Don't mention it to wifey."

"Oh!"

"You told her at lunchtime that I'd called?"

"Yes. I'm afraid I did."

"Fair enough, lad. Just tell her we're chasing a missing canister of arsenic and are talking to all the boffins on the island."

"Right."

"Now all we want is Mrs Dutton's address, and we'll be on our way."

Chapman gave them the information and they left to rejoin the sergeants.

"They're coming," said Gardam.

Reed straightened up from the railing on which he'd been leaning and said to Berger: "How does the Chief look?"

"It's difficult to tell."

"He's a funny bloke," said Gardam.

"What's funny about him?" The question was asked in a tone that dared Gardam to criticise.

"Why, when I came into the pub to tell him Mr Green had struck oil, I expected him to be pleased . . ."

"Of course he was pleased. It was what he'd been working and praying for."

"Oh, yes? So what does he do? Swallow his beer and set off to come here? Oh, no, he settles down and orders us to take our time, and he told you not to drive fast when we did set out."

"Before I joined him," said Reed, "his sergeants used to say they always knew when he'd cracked a tricky case because he used to go broody. What they really meant was he'd seen the solution, but from then on he used to tread very carefully, making sure he didn't put a foot wrong as he gathered his proof. But this case is different."

"How?"

"You know he's been given the job of looking for a nut who's spreading botulism? This nut has already killed two people and put a score more in hospital. For all we know, those figures could be doubled by now. So where does he start? There's about fifty-five million people in this country and it could be any one of them—at least in theory."

Gardam nodded. "I reckon I'm beginning to see what you mean."

"I hope you are, mate. In less than three days, George Masters has picked up a trail. Not a strong one. Just one he reckons should be there, and so, because he's got nothing else to help him, he's started to follow it. What do you expect him to do if somebody like you comes in and says there's a possibility he's made the right choice? Jump for joy?"

"Hardly."

"Quiet satisfaction, mate, that's what it was. He just daren't rush, in case whatever it was disappeared. He's got the hunter instinct—to stalk his prey slowly and carefully, giving himself time to think as he goes."

"I get you. And that's why he's so successful?"

"That, and the fact that he's got a head on his shoulders."

"And he's a decent bloke to work for," added Reed. "As long as you have the right attitude to work, that is."

Crowther joined in. "He roasted me a few months ago."

"Have you got any scars to prove it?" asked Reed.

"No, Sergeant."

"Then he didn't roast you, and he obviously bears no malice because he asked for you and Sergeant Gardam as soon as he reached your nick."

"Quiet," growled Berger.

"We have to go to an address in Newport. Perhaps you would lead us there, Sergeant Gardam?"

"Right, sir."

"Mr Wilkin?" said Mrs Dutton. "Yes, I remember him. Stayed a week at the time Mr Chapman got married."

"That's the one, love," said Green. "We're trying to get in touch with him."

"What for? Nice, quiet gentleman he was. No trouble at all except he got wet on the beach."

"Your book will have his address in it."

"It might."

"Your guests sign in, don't they?"

"Some of them."

"You mean you don't ask them to sign?"

"The book's here in the hall. If they want to fill it in, they do. But they're not forced to."

"Did Mr Wilkin sign it?"

"I don't know, and I really haven't got time to look . . . I'm busy. I've got fourteen in this week . . ."

"We'll look for ourselves."

There was no mention of Wilkin in the exercise book which Mrs Dutton took from the drawer in the old fashioned hall-stand which graced the entrance to her house.

Green handed the book back to her. "Thanks for letting us look, love. Take my advice and ask people for addresses. It could save you trouble."

"I knew he'd be no trouble. He booked by post, you see, and sent a deposit."

"But you've destroyed his letter."

"Of course. If I kept a lot of paper about, I'd have no room for paying guests, would I?"

Green shrugged and followed Masters out of the house.

"We know his name," said Masters, "and we know his job. There can't be so many cryophysicists in the country."

"Shall you phone Lake and ask him to start the search?"

Masters nodded. "And Anderson, to get a bit of heat put under the request."

"How about talking to Harry Moller, too? These government boffins should know where specialist laboratories are located."

"A good idea, Bill. We'll go straight to the Newport police station and use their phones. Just in case Anderson and Moller are thinking of knocking off for the day by now."

"Good lord," exclaimed Green. "Is it that time? After half past five?"

As they got into the cars, Masters said to Reed: "We shall probably be on the phone for half an hour, which means we won't be back at Ryde until half past six. We'll stay here tonight."

"I'd have thought you'd be in a hurry to get back, Chief."

"I will be—tomorrow morning. but there's very little we can do now until Wilkin is located."

As they were having a drink in Yelf's before dinner, Masters announced his intention of going to the summer show after he had eaten.

"To a concert party, Chief?" asked Berger in surprise.

"Why not?"

"It doesn't seem your style."

"It isn't."

"Then why go?"

"Be your age, lad," said Green. "It's the unwinding process. What can you suggest that would be better? His Nibs wants to let down—to relax mentally. And don't pull a face, because you're coming, too."

Berger stared.

"Why not?" asked Reed. "There'll be some chorus girls with nice legs." He leaned closer to Green. "He's sure he's cracked it then?"

"If you can't feel the answer to that in your bones," replied Green, "you'll never be a jack."

Chapter 7

INSPECTOR KEITH LAKE and his two assistants were working in their shirt-sleeves when Masters and his three companions, who had left the island by the first boat in the morning, walked into the office at Scotland Yard.

"Any luck?" growled Green before he was fairly through the door.

Lake, who had got to his feet to greet them, asked: "Have you any idea just how many men there are called Stephen Wilkin in the United Kingdom?"

"At a guess," replied Green, "eighteen thousand and one."

"Quite right. We've been told about the eighteen thousand. We're waiting for news of the one."

Masters removed his jacket, put it on a hanger, and placed pipe, matches and a brassy tin of Warlock Flake on the desk.

"But they're not all cryophysicists," he said quietly.

"No, Chief, they're not. And I'll tell you something else they're not."

"What's that?"

"All bank clerks or shopkeepers."

"I suppose not. But you sound tetchy, Keith."

Lake perched on the corner of Masters' desk. "The trouble is, Chief, nobody has ever heard of such a job as a cryophysicist. In spite of our description of the job, sent to every area, the lads haven't grasped it. They're going for the name first. Rightly so. But if they come across a Stephen Wilkin who works for the Electricity Board shoving new wiring into houses, they come back at us. Is this the bloke? We've had enquiries about every bloody trade and occupation in the register, including an acupuncturist and a Stefanie Wilkin who's a geophysicist."

Masters grinned. "I'm not surprised."

"Neither am I," said Reed. "I'd never heard of a cryophysicist myself until yesterday. I don't reckon I'm the only ignorant bastard in the force."

Lake scratched his head. "Neither had I, but the Chief's explanation was crystal clear . . ."

He was interrupted by the internal phone.

"Detective Chief Superintendent Masters' office." Lake seemed to enjoy his temporary occupation as Masters' staff officer, despite its frustrations.

"Yes, sir, he's back. Yes, sir. I'll tell him."

Lake put the phone down. "The Assistant Commissioner Crime would like to see you straight away, Chief."

Masters put on his jacket again. As he was leaving, he said to Green: "Have another word with Harry Moller, please, Bill. See if he's come up with any suggestions as to where we might find this character."

Green agreed, and Masters went to see Anderson.

"You're certain you've fathomed this, George?"

"As certain as I can be at this stage, sir. Short of finding him—and the evidence, of course."

"That's good, because there's been another outbreak."

"How many people affected?"

"Three. Here in London. Fish this time—mackerel fillets. Giles Convamore is coping, and he thinks there's no immediate danger, but they are all elderly people and heaven knows if they've got the stamina to survive."

Masters sat silent for a moment, and then said: "This longshot of mine, sir . . . I think it will come off. If not, I can think of very little else I can do, short of placing guards in every one of the Redcoke shops."

"To nab the chap if he tries to place any more adulterated tins?"

"That's right, sir. How else can I get him? Every police force in the country is trying to find somebody with a grudge against Redcoke. I'm not allowed to enlist the help of the public lest I cause a panic. John Stratton, the boss of Redcoke, is playing along with us as you know. And that is as far as I can go without playing my own hunches. I've played this one on the Isle of Wight, and all the signs are that we've hit the target. From the beginning we decided we were looking for a scientifically knowledgeable man who would also have laboratory technician's training. We also wanted a man who had access to food contamination by the sea . . ."

"Why the sea?"

"Because the waters of the northern hemisphere are the biggest source of type E botulism. Furthermore, sir, seawater will eat away at the metal of a tin can and, at a weak spot, perforate it enough to allow the entry of a spore."

"I see."

"So I knew what I wanted, and I believe I've got it. Certainly I've got the name of a man who is a scientist and whose branch of science necessitates the use of a well-equipped laboratory. And that man was combing a beach, helping to handle poison canisters. But besides poison canisters all manner of things were coming ashore."

"Including tinned food?"

"According to the local police, yes, sir."

"I can understand your being confident, George. It has all the hallmarks of success. Have you located this Wilkin chap yet?"

"No, sir. But Lake is having the country combed for him."

"Would the Department of Trade know all the laboratories that deal with very low temperature work?"

"We can ask them, sir."

"Department of Industry?"

"We'll try everybody, sir."

"Good. Because I suppose the aircraft people are also interested in that sort of research to help determine factors of metal fatigue."

"Quite right, sir. And the oil people and natural gas transporters."

"Right, George. Go to it. And good luck."

"Thank you, sir."

"And tell Wanda my missus wants the two of you for dinner again as soon as you can leave the baby in somebody else's care for an hour or two."

"I'll tell her, sir."

*

Green said, as soon as Masters rejoined him, "Harry Moller has been asking questions among all the leading boffins that he knows. None of them has ever heard of Wilkin."

"Is he suggesting our information is wrong?"

"I asked him that. He said not at all. So far, he has established that Wilkin is not one of your actual top flight researchers that all the university departments know by name and refer to when the need arises."

Masters accepted a cup of coffee from one of Lake's subordinates and set it down on the desk.

"Does that bug you—what Moller said?" asked Green.

Masters leaned back in his chair and clasped his hands behind his head. "Not in the least. On the contrary, in fact."

Berger asked incredulously: "You mean it's a good sign, Chief?"

"Evidentially, no."

"What the hell does that mean?" asked Green.

"Simply that it would not be good evidence in Court."

"That's a fine answer."

"To me personally, it is. In reply to Berger's question, I merely want to point out that I have formed a mental picture of Wilkin."

"We heard he was a thin, nervous sort of chap. according to young Chapman."

"About thirty. That conjures up a picture, but not the mental one I formed. I got the impression that he was the sort of chap born to be the perennial assistant. One who would never make it to the top in his own right."

"How can you possibly say that?"

"It's probably an illogical feeling, and I would have been quite disappointed if you'd told me he was a high flyer in some esoteric branch of physics."

"Would you now?"

Masters sat forward. "Come on, Bill, you must form your own mental pictures. A thin, nervous chap! And he must be an embittered little man, too, otherwise he wouldn't be trying to ease a grudge against Redcoke by killing off people he's never seen or heard of. Thin, nervous, embittered—doesn't that cause you to envisage him in such a way that you would be disappointed to learn he was an outgoing leader in his particular field?"

"I suppose so."

"That's why what you told me doesn't bug me—to use your own term. It helps, to know that the chap I'm after conforms to my picture of him."

"You could argue that anything you hear is good, Chief," said Reed. "I'd like to bet you're prepared to say that having no leads in this case—to begin with—was a distinct benefit."

"Of course he is," grunted Green. "And why not? It caused us to hare off to the Isle of Wight because we had nowhere else to go for honey. If we hadn't done that we might have been bogged down for months, with people dying like flies."

"Talking of which," said Masters, "there's been another outbreak here in London, involving three elderly people."

"And we're sitting around here doing sweet fanny," grated Green.

Masters took up the cooling cup of coffee. "It's irritating, I know, Bill, but all we can do is wait. Everybody have an early lunch and be ready to move as soon as we do get word."

It was three o'clock in the afternoon when Moller was announced and then shown up to Masters' office. He looked hot and excited. Green, who was sitting looking through Lake's diary, glanced across and said: "Been running, Doc?"

"I really think I have," admitted Moller.

"Hot news then is it?"

"At last."

"Sit down," said Masters, rising to draw up a chair for Moller. "Can we get you anything? Tea, or iced lemonade from one of the machines?"

"Nothing, thank you." He sat down. "I've located your Stephen Wilkin."

"Where?" demanded Green, moving over to join them.

"Not far," gasped Moller, fanning himself with a file cover he had picked up from the desk. "Just the other side of Kew."

"Mr Lake," called Masters. "Locate Reed and Berger and tell them we shall need the car straight away."

Green offered Moller a cigarette. Masters said: "You'd better tell us everything you can, Doctor. I like to be as well briefed as possible."

Moller grinned: "You don't have to tell me. I reckon you know more about botulism now than old Giles Convamore and myself."

"Don't butter him up," pleaded Green. "Tell us about Wilkin."

"Ah, yes. He's a technical assistant . . ."

"Only an assistant?" asked Green.

"Go to the labs in somewhere like Cambridge," retorted Moller, "and all the assistants are doctors of this and doctors of that. It merely means they're not departmental heads."

"But they're not just fetchers and carriers?"

"By no means. They do research off their own bats, but it is usually guided by somebody else and not haphazard or of their own choosing."

"I see."

"He works for a private research firm called Locklabs Limited. The managing director is Tom Lockyer—quite a leading light in a commercial sort of fashion."

"Just one moment," interrupted Masters. "A private firm? A private research firm?"

"Yes."

"In competition with places like the National Physical Laboratory?"

"Good heavens," said Moller, "didn't you know that we have private research labs?"

"Attached to big manufacturing companies," said Masters. "But not operating alone."

"I'll explain if you have time to listen."

"Please. Go ahead."

"Say you were a big kipper-manufacturer and you invented a modern way of curing your kippers which didn't involve smoking them over oak sawdust fires, you would find that your sales would drop off because the kippers hadn't got the traditional smokey flavour. So you have to have a smoke flavour. But you don't keep a lab full of food technicians and flavour chemists just for that. No, you go to a firm which specialises in solving that sort of problem.

You pay them a fee and they produce you a flavour. They may even manufacture it and sell it to you from then on. That's much cheaper than keeping a load of technical staff doing nothing, in case you want to produce a duck-flavoured sausage in five years,' time."

"Do they actually make smoke flavour?" asked Green.

"And how! Where do you think you can get oak sawdust these days? That's just one example of a private lab. But say you were a chap who was building oil rigs for the North Sea fields, and you wanted to know the best coating to put on the legs to stop them from rusting, you would have to employ private research. You wouldn't be a paint manufacturer yourself, so you would have neither the right specialists nor the laboratory for doing the testing. You would approach a private company researching in that field and they would either test all the coatings available and recommend the best, or they would start from scratch and produce you a new, modern, effective product. But you would have to pay for the formula."

"So these companies just do jobs they are hired to do?"

"Not at all. They have their own areas of ongoing research, producing answers and patents that they sell world-wide. The paint man who produces an effective coating for North Sea oilrigs may equally well sell his formula or a derivative of it to an American wanting to put rigs in the waters of the Gulf of Mexico."

"I see. British inventiveness doing its stuff."

"In a small way. We're rather good at it actually, though we never seem to have enough funds to capitalise on it."

Green gave a grunt of disgust and Reed came in. "All ready, Chief. I don't know where we're going, so I've had her filled up."

"Thank you. We're just coming." Masters turned to Moller. "If you could spare the time to come along . . . what I mean is, we shall all be at sea in a laboratory, and I don't want this particular fish to wriggle off the hook because I'm too ignorant to find the evidence prosecuting counsel will need."

Moller looked delighted. "If there's room in your barouche . . .?"

"Bill Green and I are only little 'uns. We take up barely half of the back seat."

Moller laughed, and they rose to go.

Tom Lockyer was a pleasant man, which Masters appreciated very much. It made the job of going into the company premises and doing what had to be done that much easier. He had harboured hopes that he would not be required to use the authority with which he was always armed. Ready-use warrants, taken out in the name of the Commissioner, were for infrequent use and Masters rarely found need for them. Lockyer was the sort of man who seemed intrigued at their visit and was not prepared to obstruct them unless he was given good cause.

"Detective Chief Superintendent Masters?" Lockyer came from behind his desk, hand outstretched in greeting—"I've never had the pleasure of meeting you, but those of my acquaintances who have, have found it an exhilarating experience."

"Thank you, sir. This is Detective Chief Inspector Green . . ."

"Whom I *have* met," said Lockyer, "or rather whom I have seen before. I was on a jury once where he told a rather bumptious young barrister that the villain he was defending was a right Basquinade and then went on to explain—after protests—that the man had been born on the more slippery slopes of the Pyrenees."

Masters smiled. "It's a habit of his. Was the barrister satisfied with the explanation?"

"No, but the judge was, though he said he would prefer the simpler Basque. The jury got the message, however."

"Aye, well," said Green enigmatically, "some of these young barristers have no respect for the Law, with a capital L."

"As represented by you?" Lockyer grinned and turned to see Moller in the doorway. "By jove, it's Harry Moller, isn't it? A government functionary now, I hear."

"Would I be in my present company otherwise? How are you, Tom?"

So it was a happy party. The two sergeants had been left outside with the car, as Masters had thought it best not to overwhelm Lockyer with a show of force. It had been a wise decision. Had there been more bodies present, the atmosphere could well have not been as co-operative as, from the outset, it promised to be.

"What can I do for you, gentlemen?" asked Lockyer as soon as the greetings were over.

"You will have heard that there have been several, almost simultaneous, outbreaks of botulism, Mr Lockyer."

"Nasty. It looks like becoming an epidemic."

"Not if we can prevent it, sir."

"You are dealing with it? That surprises me. I'd have thought it was a job for doctors and health authorities and . . . well, chaps like Moller here. But perhaps that is why . . .!"

As Lockyer's sentence tailed off, Masters said: "Normally, what you have just said would be correct. But the outbreaks are in widely different parts of the country and, as I said, virtually simultaneous. As botulism is so rare a disease—usually occurring about once in twenty years in this country—it was felt there was something either mysterious or sinister about the present crop of incidents."

"I see. And when things are mysterious or sinister, the police are called in, is that it?"

"The very senior police," interjected Moller.

"Of course. So where do I fit in? I presume you have approached me concerning the laboratory. But surely the government's resources are big enough to cope, though we shall be willing to help if at all possible."

There was a little silence, with Lockyer looking from one to the other of his visitors. Then—

"Mr Lockyer," said Masters slowly. "I may have misled you by not stating the reason for this visit as soon as we came into your office."

"Misled me? How?"

"We are here to seek your help, certainly, but not in the way you appear to think. We do not wish to avail ourselves of your laboratory facilities, but to establish whether or not they have been misused by one of your employees."

"You're going round every lab in the country making an inspection? Well, that seems a reasonable step to take, I suppose, but it's going to be a hell of a long and tedious job."

"No, sir. We believe your lab has been used, unbeknown to you, for criminal purposes."

Lockyer's mouth opened in surprise. For a moment he was speechless, then he seemed to recover his faculties. "I won't say that your statement is rubbish, Mr Masters, because you are obviously serious—sincere, even. But I have to say that I believe you to be mistaken. It is inconceivable that these laboratories could have been used for a criminal act. Botulism is a disease. We have nothing to do with disease and bacteria here. We are a physics team, not a team of physicians."

"Perhaps—by way of explanation—I should tell you a story," said Masters. "A story in which all the facts are true."

"I'm certainly willing to listen if it will throw some light on your suspicions of my company."

"Let me ask if you know anything about botulism?"

"Only what I've read in the papers and heard in the news programmes."

"Then you will not know that there are several types of botulism, designated by letters of the alphabet. One of the rarest is type E. Yet this is the type that Dr Moller has isolated from the cans of food eaten by all those who are now suffering from the disease."

"That must have been a bit of a hurdle for you," said Lockyer, now fully interested.

"It looked as though it might be at first, but we know that type E, though rare in Britain, is rife throughout the waters of the northern hemisphere."

"Waters? You mean seas and oceans?"

"Basically, yes."

"So you deduced that the bug itself came from the sea?"

"We have established that as a certainty. We have also established that the botulism has been introduced into tins of food under anaerobic conditions. You know what they are, Mr Lockyer?"

"Of course."

"So our man had to have the theoretical knowledge to know that anaerobic conditions are vital. He also had to have the practical laboratory skills to carry out his work successfully."

"Agreed," said Lockyer. "Laboratory facilities would be needed. Indeed it would take a good technician with a lot of modern equipment at his disposal to undertake such a task and pull it off. But I still don't see why you have descended on Locklabs."

"You will," grunted Green.

"I'm listening."

"I stressed the botulism came from the sea. But it had to find conditions to its liking before it could produce its exotoxin. The most likely place for it to find those conditions was in a tin of food —preferably a tin of fish, because it has a predilection for fish."

Lockyer nodded to show he understood.

"Such a tin of fish would probably have been in the water for some time. Seawater, as you know, will eat metals away. We think our tin had been in the sea long enough for the salt to find a weak spot on the surface of the metal . . ."

"Probably where sand and grit had worn the surface tinning off," agreed Lockyer.

"Quite. Only a minute hole would be needed—one scarcely discernible, even with a magnifying glass, and small enough to self-seal with solidified juices from the contents once the spore had entered. Once a spore entered under those conditions, it would multiply."

Lockyer nodded.

"Our next thought was that the tin would have to be retrieved from the water. While considering this, it was as well to question how it would get into the water in the first place."

"Lost overboard from a ship, presumably."

"Quite. And then, after a time, washed up on some shore to be found by somebody who made use of it as a source of virulent botulism for contaminating other tins of food."

"Haphazardly? It's fiendish."

"That's roughly how we described the operation," conceded Green, fishing out a crumpled packet of Kensitas. "Mind if we smoke in here, Mr Lockyer?"

"Go ahead." Lockyer pushed an ashtray across the desk.

Masters, glad of Green's interruption, in so far as it removed the need to connect the previous bit of his narrative with the next bit, continued his explanation.

"You may recall that last autumn there were several bouts of exceptionally severe weather in the Channel and generally off the south coast."

"The Fastnet disaster?"

"That was part of it, I believe. What I am sure about is that a number of small coasters got into difficulties and some even sank. Those disasters were recalled in the spring of this year when, some six months after the sinkings, whales started to die of poisoning."

"I do remember that," said Lockyer, "because one was washed up on the beach at Becton Bunny."

"Where?" demanded Green.

"Becton Bunny. On the Hampshire coast between Barton and Milford, not far from Christchurch. We have a cottage down there. That's why I can remember the details so well."

"I see."

"Yes. I recall now that another two were washed up on the Isle of Wight which is only just opposite our little place."

"Funny you should mention the Isle of Wight . . ." began Green, and then looked across at Masters to indicate that he could pick up the cue. But Masters did not do so, directly. Instead, he said: "The craft which went down were obviously well-provided with food, and much of it would break loose and get scattered about, so that the sea could get to work on the tins. Besides contaminating them, it would eventually wash them ashore somewhere when the wind and tides were setting in the right direction."

"The spring gales washed them ashore?"

"Together with other items from the cargoes that had been lost. At least one of those ships was carrying dangerous chemicals in canisters. And those canisters were washed ashore with the tins of food."

Lockyer grimaced. "That's right. I remember the poisons coming ashore."

"Arsenic trichloride, amino methyl propanol and phenyl

benzanine," said Masters. "All stuff that had to be handled with care and, if possible, by experienced scientists."

"I should think so. People who find things on beaches are quite naturally inquisitive and anybody getting too nosey with canisters of the poisons you have named wouldn't last long enough to make a choice as to whether they wanted to be buried or cremated."

Masters nodded his agreement. "Consequently, when those drums started to come ashore on the Isle of Wight, the authorities there roped in every scientist they could lay their hands on to identify the poisons for the police and firemen who were faced with the task of making the beaches safe."

Masters looked straight at Lockyer. "You see where we are getting, sir?"

Lockyer nodded. "You've married up a number of the scientists from among whom you expect to find a culprit with the source of the virulent botulism."

"Quite. We have reason to believe that one of the men who helped, picked up a can of food. We believe he has enough scientific knowledge to recognise its potential for harm, and we believe he has the facilities of a modern laboratory at his disposal."

Lockyer made no comment. Moller cleared his throat apologetically and Green crushed out the butt of his cigarette. At last—

"You think those laboratory facilities are in this building." It was a flat, spiritless statement.

"Yes, Mr Lockyer, I do."

"What makes you so sure?"

"One of your employees on holiday at the time of the gales was staying at a guest house on the Isle of Wight. It so happened that another young scientist—an industrial chemist—lived in that house. The chemist was rounded up to help on the beaches, but it was a most inconvenient time for him because he was just about to be married. Your man offered to stand in for him on the beaches . . ."

"Good lord! You are saying that one of my people deliberately set himself out to find a tin of contaminated food . . .?"

"No, sir. I am doubtful whether the idea ever entered his head at that time. I am sure he just picked up a tin of food that the firemen

158

had missed and probably slipped it inside the parka he would be wearing on so cold and windy a beach as he located the drums and pronounced on their safety. He forgot it, I expect, till he got back to his digs, and then didn't bother to return it to the dump. When he came away, he probably brought it with him."

"For what reason?"

"Who can say? As a scientist he might be interested in some aspect of the effects of sea water."

"Highly probable. We, here, are deeply involved in the effects of the elements on materials in everyday use. But you haven't yet told me the name of the man—I assume it is a man?—whom you suspect."

"A cryophysicist called Stephen Wilkin."

"We certainly employ him," agreed Lockyer. "And he is an assistant in the cryo lab."

"I have told you as much as I think I can safely tell you without prejudicing the case," said Masters. "So now we would like your permission to investigate further. You keep a list of holiday dates, I suppose?"

"Naturally."

"In that case, would you please allow DCI Green to check it to make sure that Wilkin was absent from the laboratory at the relevant time?"

"Nothing easier . . ." Lockyer stretched out his hand to press the button to summon his secretary and then exclaimed: "Good heavens, look at the time. It's gone six. Everybody will have left ages ago." He got to his feet. "I think I can manage to find the book myself. We are not so big an organisation that we have yielded cost efficiency to the administrative maws of water-tight compartments."

As soon as Lockyer was out of the office, Moller said to Masters: "Don't be too hard on him. This will be a great blow to him—commercially as well as . . ." "He's coming back," mumbled Green, getting to his feet to take the book that Lockyer was bringing with him.

"It was very much to the fore," he said quietly. "It is the high holiday season now, so I suppose it is in constant daily use."

Green leafed through the hard-backed ledger. After a moment or two he looked up and said to Masters: "Away for the week." Keeping his forefinger on the relevant entry, he passed it across for the Chief Superintendent to see.

"Get a photocopy of that page," counselled Masters. "There's no need to impound the book itself."

The atmosphere had changed. Now that the Yard men had started to gather material evidence a sombreness had descended on the gathering.

"We shall need to inspect the cryogenics laboratory, sir."

"There will be nobody there now."

"Nobody staying on to take late readings?"

"We try to avoid that. It costs a lot of money in overtime. By and large, readings are taken at timed intervals, and I'm pleased to say that most scientific men are prepared to come back at specified times to take readings when they are engaged in a project that necessitates them."

"So there are keys available?"

"We have a man on the door all night. He has keys to all the labs. He lets people in."

"Without question?" asked Green.

"He wouldn't let a stranger in, of course. But he knows everybody who works here. That's not quite as irresponsible as it may sound to you, because though all our work is important research, none of it is categorised by any of the Ministries, for example. An ordinary intruder would learn little from a visit to any of our labs. Really important papers are locked in the safes overnight, and they include bench diaries on any original work that's going on."

Green grunted and got to his feet.

"The photocopier is in the general office," Lockyer told him. "It will be switched off at the plug. After you've used it, please switch off again and leave the book alongside it."

"Ta!"

Masters said: "You are being very helpful and understanding Mr Lockyer."

"Helpful, perhaps, because I want to see this business cleared up. And I'm still living in hope that you are mistaken. But understanding, no. I do not understand it, Mr Masters, and I don't think I need tell you I am as near distress over this whole affair as I have been at any time over anything affecting my professional life. Apart from the damage it may do Locklabs—which probably won't matter at all, because the firm can recover—I am concerned about Stephen Wilkin."

"You like him?"

"Not very much. In fact, I probably dislike him."

"Why?"

"Probably because I did not take to him when he first came—for his first interview. Obviously he had good qualifications, otherwise we wouldn't have looked at him. But when I saw him that first time, my immediate reaction was to turn him down. After he'd gone I began to think how unfair and, indeed, unwise, my attitude was. He was far from prepossessing physically. In my day we would have called him weedy. But I asked myself whether that was a good reason for discarding him immediately. He was obviously possessed of the application and mental stamina necessary to take a good degree, and if every employer he met turned him down, out of hand, simply because he hadn't a personality that appealed immediately . . ."

"Was this his first job, then?" asked Green.

"No. His second. He came to us from a dead-end job—as far as research physics was concerned—in a small firm making traditional electric batteries."

"So you took him on out of sympathy?"

"I like to think not. I've tried to flatter myself I made a rational decision, devoid of sentiment."

"Was your choice justified?" enquired Masters.

"Until I heard what you had to tell me today, I would have said that I had engaged a hard worker who would never reach any dizzy heights."

"Did he get on well with his colleagues here?"

"In the lab he was very quiet and fussy. Outside he did not socialise at all. He was, you see, a mother's boy."

"No father? No wife or girl friends?"

"That's it. He lost his father when he was a boy. Mother brought him up tied tight to her apron. I could tell that immediately I met him, but I had hopes that coming down here on his own and living in digs would improve matters. I think it did, a bit, and he began to get a taste for freedom or solitude, whichever way you look at being alone."

"He went to the Isle of Wight alone."

"That surprised me a bit, because last autumn he bought a flat and brought his mother down here to live with him. He then reverted to the old, reserved Wilkin he had been when he first arrived. Why he went away without her is a mystery to me."

"You've met Mrs Wilkin?"

"No, no. He never comes to any of the firm's social functions and I don't inflict on my staff invitations to dinner with the boss."

"But he definitely began to come out of his shell before his mother joined him?"

"That is my belief. I thought I detected a definite lessening of his nervousness and I can recall Dewer—that's Wilkin's departmental head—saying that the man was getting frisky. He'd banged his thumb, I believe, and exhibited quite a repertoire of blue language."

"They do, that type," said Green. "You ought to hear some of your actual gay boys swear."

"They can hold their own?"

"More than that. They often use it gratuitously. I've always put it down to the fact that they want to prove they're tough."

"I see."

Masters asked: "Where did Wilkin come from?"

"Leicester."

"Was that where he was living or where he was born?"

"Oh, where he was living. I can't remember where he was born."

Masters looked at Green. "Ask Reed to tell Lake to concentrate there, would you please?"

Green left the office.

"Now," said Moller, "could we go to the lab, please, I'd like to see what there is there that he could have used."

"Wait for Green," said Masters.

When the DCI returned, Lockyer led the way to the cryo lab. Stuck with sellotape on the outside of the door was a piece cut from a newspaper full-page ad. It read—

At − 10°C your skin can turn
    as white as snow

At − 20°C your fingers can freeze
    solid to metal

At − 25°C steel can shatter into
    tiny pieces

At − 30°C you can find it hard
    to breathe.

and then, added in red with a felt pen, 'YOU HAVE BEEN WARNED!'.

"Makes you feel goose-pimply just to read that," said Green. "But I suppose it's a timely warning to anybody barging in here."

"Most assuredly." Lockyer fitted his own master key and opened the door.

While the others stood just inside, looking round, Moller began to prowl.

"I understand about as much about this," said Green, "as I do about Ancient Egypt. All those dials and meters make me think of science fiction programmes on the telly."

"George!" Moller sounded excited. He waited until the others joined him.

"Ultrasonic apparatus?" said Lockyer. "It's a modern piece, but by no means rare. What excites you so much about it?"

Moller replied: "George said Wilkin would just pick up a tin on the beach, forget to hand it in and then bring it back here. You said it would be a natural thing to do because your employees are professionally interested in the effect of natural forces on materials in everyday use."

"Right, I did."

"Something that has been exercising my mind," said Moller, "is how Wilkin would know his tin was contaminated with type E botulism, because type E is one of those organisms that doesn't cause tins to 'blow' and give any warning of its presence, nor does it turn the food rotten and make it inedible to the taste. In other words, it lies doggo, and short of some pretty comprehensive tests, nobody could detect it."

"Go on," said Masters. "We're more than interested. This has been one of the weak links in the chain."

Moller turned to the ultrasonic apparatus. "He used this little beauty."

"To detect the presence of botulism?" asked Green sceptically.

"No. Ultrasonic waves are an important tool of research in physics," said Moller. He turned to Lockyer. "It's your toy. Tell them how it works, because they'll want to know, down to the last detail. They're like that, and they're right to be so, because it's their thirst for knowledge that has brought us this far."

Lockyer stepped forward and laid one hand on the apparatus. "Ultrasonics are sound waves of so high a frequency that they are inaudible to humans—from twenty thousand cycles per second upwards."

"Like those things you can use for changing television channels while still sitting in your armchair? The things that drive dogs mad?"

"Very similar. Dogs can hear much higher frequencies than humans, and what they hear when those things are used must be a high-pitched, torturing scream. But that is by the way. For the most part, ultrasonic waves are produced by, quite simply, causing a solid object to vibrate at a very high frequency. These vibrations can pass through the air or through fluid."

"What object do you use?" asked Masters.

"In this one we use a quartz crystal. But other crystals can be used—those in which it is possible to excite vibrations easily."

"Using an electric current?"

"Oh, yes. But there are some pieces of apparatus involving a nickel component instead of a crystal. The nickel is energised magnetically—with the same results.

"The big thing is, as Moller has told you, there are numerous technical applications, some of which I'm sure you know of. Echo sounding, for instance . . ."

"In submarines?" asked Green.

"For submarine work, certainly. In industry they are used to test for flaws in castings and they are widely employed where glass or ceramics have to be drilled. And that is not all, by any means, but I suspect I've covered the ground Moller wanted me to."

"Thank you," said Masters. "Interesting, informative and, thank heaven, put simply enough for laymen like us to understand."

Moller took over once more.

"You heard Lockyer say that ultrasonics are used for detecting cracks in metal. As you might guess, they can be used for determining the morphology of any hole in metal."

"Here we go again," said Green. "Morphology?"

"Character, shape, size," supplied Lockyer.

"Thank you."

"So," went on Moller. "Wilkin brings his tin of food—I'll say it was caviare, just for laughs—and bungs it in this machine and switches on. He's probably testing it to see whether it is still sound and good enough to eat, because he rather fancies a bit of caviare. But, to his dismay, the machine tells him there's a hole. The screen says it is minute, probably too small to detect with the naked eye, but the machine does not lie. Bang goes his chance of a caviare supper. But wait . . ." Moller paused dramatically. "Wilkin is a conscientious scientist. He reads his journals—*New Scientist* and suchlike. He also has a fairly good memory. Some time ago there were articles in the journals about a tin of salmon that had a minute hole in the seam and which, after being eaten by four people, caused all four to contract severe botulism."

Masters nodded. "The existence of a minute hole was the trigger. Is that what you are saying?"

"That's it."

"I think you're right. It set him thinking. He went home and turned up the back numbers of his journals. Did a bit of research on botulism, in fact."

"But why?" demanded Lockyer. "Why, in heaven's name?"

"Because he'd got a grudge to ease," said Green.

"What grudge?"

"That's what we're hoping to find out, chum. It will supply the motive. Not that we have to supply one. All we have to establish is means and opportunity, but motive helps to tie the business up with a jury."

"You mean you are going to arrest him?"

"I think we shall have to," said Masters. "Quite soon, that is. There are still one or two points . . ."

He was interrupted by a loud 'Ah!' of satisfaction from Moller who had wandered away from them and was continuing his journey of inspection round the lab.

Masters turned in his direction.

"Got something else?" asked Green.

Moller was standing by a large cylinder, upright in an iron cradle. It was about five feet tall and a foot in diameter, painted black and carrying a forest of gauges, ring taps and keys screwed into the top. "Nitrogen," he said, slapping the cylinder on the shoulder, "under pressure. Filled to one hundred and seventy five bar max and with a hose take-off that can be screwed on to any bit of apparatus you like, virtually."

"Nitrogen?" said Lockyer. "What's odd about that? You'll find it in practically every working lab in the country."

"Working lab?" asked Masters.

"Where technicians actually have to do things," replied Lockyer, a little testily. "There's pressure and power there. Surely you realise that pressure hoses are necessary for all sorts of things?"

"I do, sir," replied Masters quietly. "I merely wanted to establish that Wilkin was accustomed to doing practical bench work as opposed to a deal of theory and the reading of a few dials."

"Oh, I see. Yes, he was a technician. He'd be of no use in a lab that has to earn its bread and butter commercially unless he was a dextrous man. Paper research is for government institutions and the development sections of large companies—where the living comes in, so to speak."

"Thank you." Masters turned to Moller. "I think you were going to tell us something, Doctor."

"Yes. Botulism is anaerobic, but it is quite happy with nitrogen. There's power here. Controlled power. Our friend had only to fit a syringe on the end of this line, and then he could use the power of the nitrogen to drive his culture into the contents of the tin without any air or oxygen being involved."

"In much the same way as we originally envisaged?"

"Oh, quite. But it makes it easier to know that there was nitrogen available. It doesn't make the operation foolproof, but it probably explains why he was successful on some occasions, if not on others."

"Thank you."

"Now what?" asked Green.

Masters turned to Lockyer.

"This will be distasteful, sir, but we shall have to search the lab or those sections of it where Wilkin worked. His private drawers and lockers particularly. You can, of course, be present, and Dr Moller, too, if you wish."

Lockyer shrugged. "We shall need keys. The masters and spares will be in one of the safes. I'll get them."

The two sergeants were brought in to carry out the search. Not that it was either difficult or prolonged. The locker carrying Wilkin's name in its slot contained seven tins of Redcoke foods, all of the strip variety. One was without a label. The label itself was discovered in one of the bench drawers. It had been carefully removed and lay flattened beneath several books. A phial of glue was also there."

"No syringe, Chief."

"Never mind. I want the source of the botulism. An old rusty tin or its contents sealed up in an airtight jar or something of that nature."

Moller turned to Lockyer. "Where would he keep it? It's deadly, you know. Away from oxygen . . ."

"What form would it take?"

"We don't know. A block of fish or meat or a soup made from it . . . we just don't know. Except that it must be away from oxygen or air."

It was Masters who said: "I read that a distinctive feature of type E is that it can grow and produce its toxin at four degrees centigrade—the operating temperature of a domestic refrigerator."

Lockyer grimaced. "This is a cryogenics lab," he said. "The people here have to work with very low temperatures indeed. Obviously we can't lower the temperature of the whole lab. We have cold cabinets—no, not like the local delicatessen shop. Like a meat cold store. You walk into them. They're graded. The least cold is, as Mr Masters has put it, at the temperature of a domestic refrigerator. That one is really a store-room for liquid helium and the like. We use helium in cryogenics for cooling other substances down to—well, as near to absolute zero as we need to go."

"Where is this cabinet, please?"

"Through this door."

It was unlabelled. A metal cylinder with a brass tube at each end, each tube with a screw valve and an adaptor.

"We shall have to test it, of course," said Moller, "but it is quite simple. He connects one end to the nitrogen cylinder and the other to his syringe. Then he opens both valves, gives a controlled blast with the nitrogen and hey presto. The pressure blows a little of his culture into the syringe. He closes that valve. Then he closes the other. The space vacated by the soup is occupied by nitrogen."

"He'd make this himself?"

"Nothing to it," said Lockyer. "They're standard parts. All he'd need is a soldering iron and probably some cement to make sure the solder was airtight." He turned to Moller. "I suppose you'd like a box to carry it in?"

"Yes, please. I don't fancy having that around, even though I know it would be safe if the air got at it and I didn't lick my fingers."

As they prepared to go, Masters asked for Wilkin's address. He thanked Lockyer for his help and apologised for troubling him.

They settled in the car, and Reed turned to Moller. "You didn't handle that cylinder, did you Doctor?"

"I was careful not to, and you wrapped it up."

"Good. It's just that I want to go over it for prints before you and your boyos start on it."

"Don't worry. Bring it round to the lab tomorrow morning, still wrapped up. You can then do your stuff before we open it."

"You'll put it on a nitrogen cylinder?" asked Masters.

"Just as he did. A teaspoonful of the contents will be more than enough for our tests."

"Eight o'clock," said Green. "Time for a drink and food. When are you picking the boyo up, George?"

"It will have to be tonight," said Reed. "If we wait until tomorrow he'll arrive at the lab and know immediately we're on to him."

"Not quite," said Masters. "Tomorrow is Saturday. He won't be going to the lab. Or at least he shouldn't." He turned to Green. "You see the point, don't you, Bill?"

Green grunted. "You want to catch him red-handed. Tomorrow, being Saturday, he'll likely go off to plant some of his doings. We keep him under observation and nab him."

"It would clinch matters."

"What if he doesn't?" asked Berger.

"If he doesn't go to the shops, but goes to the lab the same applies," said Masters. "We pick him up on the job. But I don't think he will go to the lab. He won't want to attract attention to himself. He'll do his lab work at lunchtimes when he's alone, or indeed, quite openly. If there are four or five boffins beavering away in that lab who's going to notice why one of them is using various bits of apparatus that they all use frequently in the normal course of events? Besides, they are researching and experimenting. That means they can do virtually anything and nobody will be surprised." He shook his head. "No, I don't think our friend will have encountered any difficulty on that score. We shall, of course, have to talk to the colleagues he worked with. There may have been something useful they can recall."

"And if he stays at home, Chief?"

"Then we've lost nothing. We can pick him up there as soon as we are satisfied he isn't going either to the shops or the lab."

"So there's nothing doing tonight anyway?" asked Green.

"I'll have to speak to Anderson. He may think we should move immediately or, alternatively, that we should keep Wilkin under observation. I personally think there's no need, but the Home Office is involved and the AC may think it politic to get the thing over."

"There's still a lot to do, Chief," said Berger. "Those prints for instance. And we should compare them . . ."

"What with?"

"The tins in Dr Moller's laboratory."

"Sorry, Sergeant," said Moller. "They've been cleaned out of all recognition. Your only hope there is if that unlabelled tin in his locker has his prints, or if the ones with labels on have been already processed. You collected them, I suppose."

"Yes."

"You'd better let me have them, too, after you've dusted them. We'd better examine the contents."

They dropped Moller and proceeded to the Yard. Masters said to Green: "Do me a favour, Bill. While I ring Anderson at home, would you call Wanda from your office and tell her I'll be home shortly. You'll be ringing Doris, I suppose?"

Anderson listened carefully to the phoned report and then replied: "I'm not going to interfere, George, and I'll see that nobody else does. Play it your way. It is obvious that we should not forgo the chance to catch the chap *in flagrante delicto*, no matter what anybody else may think—just so long, that is, as you don't allow him to plant any more of his doctored tins. That must not happen."

Masters assured him that every care would be taken and was just putting the phone down when Green entered.

"My missus is with yours," he said. "They were expecting us for supper ten minutes ago. And Wanda tells me she's got a large, cold, prawn quiche, salad and sauté potatoes. And she's got a shelf full of beer in the fridge."

"Right. What are we waiting for?"

"But why?" demanded Doris. "Why kill people you don't know and who've never done you any harm? Kiddies, too. The man must be a lunatic."

"His buddies don't think so," replied her husband. "No, that's wrong. I don't think he's got any buddies. His colleagues. Lockyer doesn't like him much, but he works well—plods along, you know, apparently a stable character." He lifted a forkful of the prawn quiche. "By gum, love, this is good," he said to Wanda. "I hope there's another in the kitchen."

"As a matter of fact, there is. Just a small one. Made from the left-over bits."

"You really do spoil the fool," said Doris. "It's a wonder I manage to live with him after he's visited you."

Masters put his knife and fork down. "That's probably Wilkin's trouble. Being spoilt at home. Doting, possessive mother . . ."

"And a lad with a whatsit complex," added Green. "Oedipus, wasn't it?"

"Oedipus was in love with his mother," said Wanda. "In the wrong sort of way, I mean."

"That's right," agreed her husband. "The Oedipus complex is a psychoanalyst's term for an infantile fixation on the mother, whether or not the father is about. Wilkin's isn't quite like that. He falls almost into the same category as the unmarried daughter who is expected to stay at home and look after ageing parents. But not quite, as I say. He was obviously over-protected as a child by a widowed mother who was too jealous of him."

"Jealous? Oh, you mean she didn't want to lose him, too?" asked Doris.

"Right. And jealousy is a form of the same selfishness as that evinced by the ageing parents of unmarried girls. It becomes demanding—just to prove that it is still a powerful enough force to maintain the hold. And a maintained hold ossifies over the years into an indissoluble link and becomes two-way. The object assumes some of the characteristics of the subject."

"You mean they grow alike?"

"Exactly."

"Now what about that left-over quiche, love?" asked Green. "I reckon there must be an indissoluble link between that and the first one and if it has the same characteristics, then we should treat it the same."

"And eat it?"

"With relish, poppet."

Wanda laughed and got up from the table to go into the little kitchen.

"Bill," scolded his wife. "You really have no manners at all. Asking like that."

Masters laughed. "Bill's quite right. He's brought us down to earth. I shouldn't talk shop at the table."

"Particularly when the problem is no longer pressing," added Green.

"Here you are, William," said Wanda, carrying in the little quiche. "Can you eat it all? Please do if you can, because I hate having left-overs."

"Just to please you, love," replied Green, holding out his plate.

"Pig," said his wife.

As soon as Masters entered his office the next morning, Lake handed him a telex. "I thought you should see this. It came in early this morning from the Leicester police."

"Thank you. While I'm reading this, would you see if Reed and Berger are ready and check whether the DCI has got the warrant?"

"Warrant, Chief? What for? An arrest?"

"Yes. You didn't know?"

Lake shook his head. "I knew you were pretty close, of course, and I guessed you were almost there, but I didn't know for sure."

"I believe we've done it. I'll tell you the full story later. The AC will want a comprehensive report. I'd be glad if you'd do that for me."

"It'll be a pleasure."

Thank you."

Lake returned to his desk to use the internal phone. Masters read the telex and sat thoughtfully until Lake returned to him.

"You read the message, Chief?"

"Yes, thank you. File it please."

"Does it help?"

"Help? Oh yes, it helps." Masters sounded so bitter that Lake made no attempt to continue the conversation. He left Masters alone to fill his pipe, automatically, his mind on other things.

Green entered.

"Everything fixed, George."

"Right, Bill. Let's get it over."

As they made their way westwards through the Saturday morning traffic, Green said: "Something's biting you, George. What's up, chum?"

Masters waited a moment before replying.

"I'm a little puzzled as to why a chap like Wilkin, who was tied so closely to his mother, should go away on holiday by himself, as he obviously did when he went to the Isle of Wight."

Green replied immediately. "I asked myself the same thing last night after we got home from your place—in view of what you'd been saying about the ossified link with his mother."

"What conclusion did you reach, if any?"

"This may be a bit too easy for you to accept, George . . ."

"Try me."

"Wilkin came down here to get a job . . ."

"Why?" asked Berger. "If he was living all nice and cosy with mummy up in Leicester? Why go out into the hard, hard world alone?"

"A good question, lad," said Green surprisingly. "I asked that one myself. Lockyer told us he was in a dead-end job in a small firm. So what drove him out into the hard, hard world as you put it, was hard reality. He had no prospects in the firm that made batteries. He was probably badly paid, and cold economics told him he had to move if he was ever going to get a worthwhile salary."

"But would that appeal to him? Wouldn't he just go on economising and stay safe?"

"A man without his knowledge and ability might have done. But I suspect Wilkin knew his worth, and I reckon ability such as his must give rise to ambition."

Masters nodded.

"And," went on Green, "we mustn't forget that we know Wilkin is a chap who bears grudges. He'd be well aware that he wasn't getting what he was worth in Leicester. He'd have a grudge against his firm because of it."

"Anybody would."

"Right. But there was probably little he could do about it except get out. He'd do it from a different motive. Most of us would do it to please ourselves and to get more lolly. Wilkin probably did it to deprive the battery firm of his services, which they were getting on the cheap. In other words he did it to make them sorry for not paying him more."

"It's a good assessment," said Masters. "I like it."

"So." continued Green, "Wilkin started applying for jobs much more in keeping with his qualifications, and he got taken on by Locklabs. That meant he had to leave his mother and go into digs down here. I reckon he found being on his own wasn't too bad. In fact, I'd go so far as to say he grew to like it."

"Good point," said Masters. "Lockyer hinted that he seemed to be happier and was settling down better."

"Until his mother joined him," said Green.

"Why bring her down, then?" asked Berger.

"Well he would, wouldn't he? Before he left to come down here, he probably promised he'd find a house. But that doesn't matter. His Nibs is worried as to why Wilkin went off on holiday alone. All I'm saying is he got to like it on his own when his mother wasn't with him, and he made up his mind that after she rejoined him he was going to go about without her. That explains how he could trot about the country buying and placing his tins in Derby, Somerset, Colchester, Bournemouth and wherever. He took lone trips and lone holidays."

"I think you've set my mind at rest on that score, Bill. Thanks." Masters glanced at his wristwatch. "Hurry it up a bit, Reed. It's after nine o'clock and I don't want Wilkin to be out and about before we get there."

"Sorry, Chief. All the grockles are out. They never look at a car all week, but come Saturday and Sunday—especially when the weather's like this—they're out getting their full road-fund's worth."

It was a new maisonette, on the ground floor.

"Looks all quiet, Chief," said Reed. "The milk's still on the doorstep."

"There'll be another way out—through the kitchen most

likely," said Masters. "Go round there, please, Berger. And while you're there see if he has a car."

"Right, Chief."

They gave him a moment or two to get down the narrow concrete path, but there was no need to knock. The door opened and a small, shrewish woman enquired their business.

"We're police officers, ma'am. We would like to speak to Mr Wilkin."

"Police officers? Dressed like that? I've been watching you through the window. You're up to no good."

"Mr Wilkin, please."

"He's not in."

"Then please tell me where he is."

"He's out, I tell you."

"Chief!"

It was Berger. Reed stepped back to look along the path. "He's here," shouted Reed.

They trooped along the side of the little house. "A moped," said Reed. "He was just about to be off."

"Glad we caught you in time, son," said Green heavily. "You weren't about to go to the grocer's, I hope?"

"What if I was?"

"You were?"

"I was going for a run down to the coast."

"Any particular place?"

"Nowhere in particular."

"No? Brighton perhaps? Or some other town with a Redcoke store and about fifty thousand holiday-makers doing their weekend shopping." Green took him by the arm. "Inside, Mr Wilkin. We want a word with you."

"You leave my Stevie alone!"

Mrs Wilkin was standing at the back door, watching closely.

"Inspect the panniers and his bag," Masters said to Reed. "Handle anything there very carefully."

"What do you want with my boy?"

"We want to talk to him, madam, so please stand aside."

"I won't. This is my house."

"No, it's not, mother," asserted Wilkin. "It's mine. Please get out of the way."

There was only one room besides kitchen and bedrooms. Wilkin led the way in. "See his mother stays out," said Masters to Berger. "I don't want any tantrums from her."

'Right, Chief.' Berger turned in the room doorway to block it to Mrs Wilkin. "Not you, madam. You'd be best in the kitchen."

"I want to know what's going on."

"That's probably your trouble," said Berger, closing the door. "You come and make yourself a cup of tea and stay out of things."

"I'm going in there."

"You're not, you know. And if I have any bother I'll handcuff you to the kitchen table." He ushered her out of earshot of the voices in the room.

Masters and Green sat at the modern dining-table which occupied one end of the room. Somehow they managed to get the small Wilkin between them—overpowering him with the mere presence of their bulk.

"Now, Mr Wilkin," began Masters, "you can save time and tell me exactly where you put your contaminated tins, so that we can recover them, or we can go into matters in detail."

"I don't think I know what you're talking about."

Masters glared at him. "Let me make my position quite clear, Mr Wilkin. Five days ago I was told that somebody was criminally contaminating tins of food with botulism. I was ordered to find that somebody. When I first heard of it, I wondered what sort of a fiend he could be who would poison food so that people—all strangers to him—should be taken seriously ill, some to die. Yes, to die. Children. Who would kill innocent young girls and boys?

"I supplied my own answer, and I vowed that once I caught up with that man . . . well, shall we just say that I am interviewing you here in your own house rather than in a police station because here I can't be said to be holding you. I'm not arresting you and I'm not charging you, so you can't get on a phone and ask for a lawyer, and I don't have to warn you to watch your tongue. Because I'm going to have the story, Mr Wilkin, in every detail, and you stay right where you are until you do tell me. No food, no drink, nothing. My sergeants have your mother, so she can't do anything to help you. So now, talk."

"I have nothing to say."

"Have it your way. Detective Chief Inspector Green and I can take it in turns to go out for a drink or a bite to eat or to stretch our legs."

"I want to go to the lavatory."

"Hard luck, chum," said Green. "You can do it in your pants. There are four of us here, and we can call on as many more as we want to take a turn watching you."

"Thanks for the reminder, Bill," said Masters. "Call Inspector Lake and his two men. Tell them to stand by to relieve us at six o'clock this evening. The phone's in the hall."

Green got to his feet and left the room. As he did so, Reed came in.

"Four tins, Chief. All strip cans. In his bag."

"After the DCI has finished with the phone, call Dr Moller at the forensic laboratory. Ask him to send a messenger for them."

"Right, Chief."

Masters turned to Wilkin. "How long do you think it will take the forensic laboratory to find out that you've tampered with those tins—removed their labels and injected them with that concoction I found in a cylinder in your laboratory? Come on, Mr Wilkin, you're a research physicist. How long would it take you to find the hole with an ultrasonic apparatus? How long to compare your finger-prints on the tins we've just found with those on that cylinder and on the other contaminated tins. We've got science on our side, too."

Green came in. "All fixed."

"How did you . . .?"

"How did we what, Mr Wilkin? Get on to you?"

Wilkin nodded miserably.

"Easy," said Green, as if to spare Masters the embarrassment of having to reply. "You made the mistake of using type E botulism. Comes from the sea, doesn't it? Or didn't your text books tell you that? Well, all we had to do was find some cranky scientist who'd done something like hauling canisters out of the sea on the Isle of

Wight and we were half-way home. The things in your lab told us the rest."

"Come on now, Mr Wilkin, let's get it over with."

"I want to go to the lavatory."

"Not yet. Why were you trying to ruin Redcoke Stores?"

No reply.

"Was it because Redcoke in Leicester had prosecuted your mother for shoplifting?"

Green raised his eyebrows. Masters, realising Green had not been told of the telex, nodded.

"No," said Wilkin fiercely, "it wasn't."

"But your mother was prosecuted for shoplifting, wasn't she?"

"Yes, but it wasn't just because they'd taken her to court."

"Why then?"

"You wouldn't understand," said Wilkin bitterly.

"I might. Tell me."

"Don't you people bloody well see what happened? I'd got away from her. Got down here on my own. You've no idea how that felt. No, she wouldn't come with me. She'd never leave Leicester. I was ruining her life by coming here. She tried to blackmail me into staying. But I came and for the first time in my life I knew what freedom was. Just to be able to do some things that I wanted . . . it was marvellous."

"Go on," said Masters quietly.

"And then Redcoke prosecuted her. Can't you see what happened? 'I can't stay here, now. I'm ruined. You've got to give me a home with you, where people don't know me. I'll never be able to lift my head up again in Leicester', and so on and so on." Wilkin looked up with tears in his eyes. "You've no idea what that did to me. I couldn't refuse her, and I was back again, back in all the dreary old nagging routine I'd broken away from. And that's what Redcoke did. They didn't only prosecute my mother, they robbed me of the only freedom and happiness I'd ever known. Do you wonder I hated them?"

He collapsed, head on hands, sobbing on the table. Masters looked at Green, who said: "Come on, Mr Wilkin, you wanted to go to the lavatory."

"It's too late."

Masters strode to the door. "Reed." When the sergeant appeared, he said: "Take Wilkin to the bathroom to clean himself up and let him change his clothes. After that I want him taken to the Yard. We'll charge him there."

"Where will you be, Chief?"

"I'll ring for another car for you and Berger and Wilkin. I'll drive the DCI back in the Rover."

"Right, Chief. You got something important to do?"

"As a matter of fact I have. I want to ring Stratton—the managing director of Redcoke—to tell him that he can test all his tins with an ultrasonic apparatus and then put them back on the shelves. And while you're at it, Reed, try to get Wilkin to tell you in which shops he actually placed his contaminated tins."

"Right, Chief. See you later."

"And that," said Green as Masters pulled away, heading for London, "is that. Poor little sod. He wanted his freedom. I wonder how much freedom he'll get, spending the next decade three to a cell in one of the monarch's maisonettes?"

Masters didn't reply. All he could think of was a child dying in fear, throat too paralysed to cry out. And he cursed Wilkin silently, savagely, knowing that had that child been his, Wilkin, too, might now be dead.

Chapter 8

WHEN MASTERS AND Green reached the Yard, they found a message from Anderson awaiting them. He had recalled the members of the original conference held in his office a few nights earlier. He wished them to join him as soon as they arrived.

Anderson, Convamore, Moller and Wigglesworth were awaiting them. Anderson wasted no time in calling the meeting to order.

"George, all we know is that you have found your man and have arrested him. The rest of us here want to know the full story and your proposals for cleaning up any trouble this fellow, Wilkin, may have left behind. Because we're not out of the wood until we can be positive we have mopped up behind him."

"I think we can be confident we can clear the matter up satisfactorily, sir."

"Good. Give us the details."

Masters was about to start when there was a knock at the door and Dr Cutton of the DHSS was shown in.

"Sorry if I've kept you all waiting," he said toothily. "Affairs of State, you know."

Masters heard Green groan loudly, and silenced his subordinate with a look. Green sucked his partial denture with a disgusting wheeze like that of the piston in a pump that has run dry. It was lost on Cutton, who loftily took his seat and looked around as if giving the assembly permission to carry on.

Masters' account was listened to in silence. Everybody there, including Cutton, seemed to appreciate that though unmentioned, the investigative skill behind the baldly-stated events was of a very high order. It was Wigglesworth who, at the end, said: "Are you telling us, George, that this chap Wilkin went to those lengths to kill people unknown to him, just because his mother had gone to live with him?"

"That is the excuse he has given us."

"It's a bit thin as a motive, isn't it?"

"Hatred? Perhaps so, but it is one of the stronger emotions all of which, as you must know, have driven men to murder before now. Love, jealousy, greed, lust . . . they've all caused tragedy."

"Right, young Masters," boomed Convamore. "The longest pleasure."

"What's that?" demanded Anderson. "The longest pleasure?"

"Hatred. Byron said it. 'Now hatred is by far the longest pleasure; Men love in haste, but they detest at leisure.' "

"I see."

"Convamore is quite right," said Cutton surprisingly. "And so is Masters. He's produced the basic motive. When prosecuting counsel gets his brief he will, of course, elaborate what Masters has given him. And he'll go to medical men for help. Any of them worth their salt will soon show him that Wigglesworth's complaint that such a motive is thin is rubbish."

"Well . . ." began Wigglesworth.

"Are you worth your salt, Doc?" demanded Green.

Cutton grinned toothily. "Trying me out are you?"

"Quoting your own words back at you."

"Right. If you'll bear with me, Anderson, I'll try to show you what I mean."

"Please go ahead."

Cutton turned to face Masters and Green. "As a medical man I should say that what you have uncovered in Wilkin, is an obsessive-compulsive neurosis. Am I right, Convamore?"

"Not exactly my line of country, but I'd say you were correct."

"Thank you. Now, we all know what an obsession is, because they commonly occur to a slight degree in all of us. But an increased feeling of compulsion to undertake some mental or physical act which is wrong or criminal is found in several kinds of psychological illness. Sometimes as, I suggest, in Wilkin's case, the obsessional trait is the outstanding feature of his illness. Because ill, he certainly is.

"What we have to appreciate is that the hereditary factor is strong in obsessional neurosis."

"Do you mean he inherited this mean streak from his mother?" demanded Green. "If so, having met her, I'd agree."

"From his mother, his father or both," went on Cutton. "The parents of people suffering from obsessive states are often found to be similarly afflicted—though not necessarily to the same degree. Meticulous, rigid routine imposed by such parents, whether imposed by discipline, or—as seems to be the case with Wilkin—by a constant nagging, whining, obstructive atmosphere, can be, however, more conducive to obsessional neurosis in offspring than hereditary endowment. But whichever the cause, the kids grow up with typical personalities.

"And this is where the motive can be seen to become less thin, Mr Wigglesworth. Children like Wilkin grow up to become sticklers for precision and detail . . ."

"As shown by the lengths he went to in preparing and placing his poisoned cans," said Masters.

"Quite. But this precision does not lead to a higher standard of work."

"He became a scientist," objected Wigglesworth.

"True. But he did not rise in his field. He was relatively unknown and had held down only unimportant jobs."

"Why?" demanded Masters, who was patently greatly interested in what Cutton had to say.

"Why? Because they become so lost in attention to detail that there is interference with the main stream of activity. I'll explain that . . ."

"Let me see if I understand. Am I right in thinking that they weigh the pros and cons of every situation so minutely that they become lost in a welter of detail so that they never reach the final conclusions and decisions?"

"Right," grinned Cutton.

"Wait a minute," said Wigglesworth. "Wilkin came to a decision and we know what the result was."

"No, no, he didn't. He didn't think the thing through properly otherwise he'd have known that his solution was wrong. He wanted to make Redcoke pay for prosecuting his mother. But his quarrel—hatred—was with his mother, not Redcoke. And to make Redcoke pay—for a perfectly legitimate action on their part—he decided to kill scores of innocent people. If the only way out of his dilemma was to kill, then the person he should have murdered would be his mother."

"Clear to me," said Anderson.

"Thank you. Now I'll just add a little rider at this point. Masters will know whether this is correct, but usually the characteristics I've ascribed to them make obsessional neurotics rigid in outlook, stubborn in character and morose in temperament."

"He's all that and more," said Green. "Stubborn? He sat and messed his pants before he'd come clean—if you'll pardon the paradox. And as for being morose—well, you wouldn't describe him as being exactly as cheerful as a linty."

"Linty?"

"Linnet," said Masters.

"I'll get on," said Cutton. "I think that the psychiatrist who advises prosecuting counsel will be at pains to point out that obsessions can usually—if arbitrarily—be divided into four parts. The common headings for these four areas are ideas, impulses, phobias and ruminations.

"Ideas are thoughts and images which are often obscene or criminal in nature and constantly recur to the patient."

"I was wondering about that point," said Masters. "I couldn't decide whether Wilkin started his campaign on the spur of the moment or whether the idea had been with him for a long time—awaiting an opportunity to develop."

"You're mixing two things up," said Cutton. "The idea will have been there, in his mind, on and off, for a long time. But remember I said impulses were the second part of an obsession. Impulses are urges to act—often to act criminally—like pushing somebody under a train or to inflict pain and then to laugh at having done so. So probably, though the idea of getting back at Redcoke had been with Wilkin a long time, the method he eventually used may have been—must have been—made on impulse, because he could not possibly have known he would have had the means of contaminating tins until he literally discovered botulism by chance."

"Thank you. I've got it clear now."

"Good. Phobias are fears. Fears of some act which the patient knows is wrong and seeks to avoid."

"Explain, please," said Anderson.

"At its simplest, a patient may develop a phobia of knives because he has a fear that he may use one to murder somebody with. He knows it is wrong to use a knife for murderous ends, but he feels he may not be able to prevent himself doing so, so he avoids knives—won't touch them, won't wash them up, or any of the usual things. That's his phobia."

"Thanks."

"Ruminations are the constant turning over of problems— problems, mark you, not ideas—in the mind. One imagines they are seeking answers to these problems and not finding them. Probably that is why Wilkin came to so disastrous a conclusion to his problem. He didn't or couldn't find the simple answer to the problem of his mother which was as easy as refusing to have her to live with him.

"Anyhow, as you will guess, these symptoms are by no means clear cut. They often overtop each other and any one of them may be the most intense. Depending upon the degree of intensity, they may upset life a little or a lot. In Wilkin, they were so severe as to make ordinary life an impossible task. Unfortunately, in these particular cases, suicide is so uncommon as to be considered atypical. Which is a pity really, because otherwise this trouble may have been avoided." He looked across at Wigglesworth. "Has that destroyed your notion that the motive was thin?"

"If it hasn't," said Convamore, "I'd like to know what would."

Masters got to his feet, anticipating the end of the meeting. Green said to him quietly: "It was a bloody good explanation, but I liked that bit of Byron's best—about hatred being the longest pleasure. I reckon that summed it up nicely."

Masters smiled his agreement.

THE PERENNIAL LIBRARY MYSTERY SERIES

Delano Ames

CORPSE DIPLOMATIQUE	P 637, $2.84
FOR OLD CRIME'S SAKE	P 629, $2.84
MURDER, MAESTRO, PLEASE	P 630, $2.84
SHE SHALL HAVE MURDER	P 638, $2.84

E. C. Bentley

TRENT'S LAST CASE	P 440, $2.50
TRENT'S OWN CASE	P 516, $2.25

Gavin Black

A DRAGON FOR CHRISTMAS	P 473, $1.95
THE EYES AROUND ME	P 485, $1.95
YOU WANT TO DIE, JOHNNY?	P 472, $1.95

Nicholas Blake

THE CORPSE IN THE SNOWMAN	P 427, $1.95
THE DREADFUL HOLLOW	P 493, $1.95
END OF CHAPTER	P 397, $1.95
HEAD OF A TRAVELER	P 398, $2.25
MINUTE FOR MURDER	P 419, $1.95
THE MORNING AFTER DEATH	P 520, $1.95
A PENKNIFE IN MY HEART	P 521, $2.25
THE PRIVATE WOUND	P 531, $2.25
A QUESTION OF PROOF	P 494, $1.95
THE SAD VARIETY	P 495, $2.25
THERE'S TROUBLE BREWING	P 569, $3.37
THOU SHELL OF DEATH	P 428, $1.95
THE WIDOW'S CRUISE	P 399, $2.25
THE WORM OF DEATH	P 400, $2.25

Francis Iles

BEFORE THE FACT	P 517, $2.50
MALICE AFORETHOUGHT	P 532, $1.95

Michael Innes

THE CASE OF THE JOURNEYING BOY	P 632, $3.12
DEATH BY WATER	P 574, $2.40
HARE SITTING UP	P 590, $2.84
THE LONG FAREWELL	P 575, $2.40
THE MAN FROM THE SEA	P 591, $2.84
THE SECRET VANGUARD	P 584, $2.84
THE WEIGHT OF THE EVIDENCE	P 633, $2.84

Mary Kelly

THE SPOILT KILL	P 565, $2.40

Lange Lewis

THE BIRTHDAY MURDER	P 518, $1.95

Allan MacKinnon

HOUSE OF DARKNESS	P 582, $2.84

Arthur Maling

LUCKY DEVIL	P 482, $1.95
RIPOFF	P 483, $1.95
SCHROEDER'S GAME	P 484, $1.95

Austin Ripley

MINUTE MYSTERIES	P 387, $2.50

Thomas Sterling

THE EVIL OF THE DAY	P 529, $2.50

If you enjoyed this book you'll want to know about
THE PERENNIAL LIBRARY MYSTERY SERIES
Buy them at your local bookstore or use this coupon for ordering:

Qty	P number	Price
postage and handling charge		$1.00
_____ book(s) @ $0.25		
TOTAL		

Prices contained in this coupon are Harper & Row invoice prices only.
They are subject to change without notice, and in no way reflect the prices at
which these books may be sold by other suppliers.

**HARPER & ROW, Mail Order Dept. #PMS, 10 East 53rd St., New
York, N.Y. 10022.**
Please send me the books I have checked above. I am enclosing $_____
which includes a postage and handling charge of $1.00 for the first book and
25¢ for each additional book. Send check or money order. No cash or
C.O.D.s please

Name_____

Address_____

City_____State_____Zip_____
Please allow 4 weeks for delivery. USA only. This offer expires 2/28/85.
Please add applicable sales tax.